a carnival of birds

pam jones

Denver, Colorado

Published in the United States by:
Spaceboy Books LLC
1627 Vine Street
Denver, CO 80206
www.readspaceboy.com

Cover art includes CC0 photo by 1899441 via Pixabay and samples from *The Garden of Earthly Delights* by Hieronymus Bosch

ISBN: 978-1-951393-29-8
First printed November 2023

"*A Carnival of Birds* is a brilliant peek inside a carousel of characters reminiscent of nostalgic American classics of the 50s, but more than this: clever transcends clever, and Jones has proven to be not only an expert in her creation of this town and its people but also a keen insight into the minds of those 'on the edge of the pit where the beast waited.' Readers will want to turn these pages just to see what predicaments Jones has in store."

— Hillary Leftwich, author of *Ghosts Are Just Strangers Who Know How to Knock* and *Aura, a memoir*

"In *A Carnival of Birds*, Pam Jones's industrious protagonist yearns to build a theme park that will bring glory and wonder into his life. With this premise, Jones plunges readers into the world of mystery and magic that is Ickack Pleasure Gardens. Jones's distinct voice carries the reader into the dark underbelly of this theme park and its madcap characters. With wit and daring, Jones carries a story that will keep readers guessing as they dive into the heart of ambition and just how far people will go to realize their dreams."

— Veronica Bane, author of *Mara, Miyuki,* and *Don't Call It an Invasion*

To John Clayton, who saw the first draft in 2011

chapter 1

A morning in June: ninety degrees before ten o'clock, California hills, dust, and, perhaps, one million people. Freddy Novak could not stop to count, but when he let himself focus, he noted that the crowd was made up of separate clusters, each made up of a woman, a man, and at least one child.

The crowd could not keep their hands off him. His former-boss-turned-publicity agent, Arnold Shake, kept Freddy wedged between two thick security men in sunglasses. Shake lagged behind to press and bat at the creases in his linen trousers; Freddy thought he gave off the impression of what a rat turned into a man might look like, negotiating a fancy suit with creeping little paws. But then, Freddy must have made a pretty picture, himself: Shake said that a unique impression, in Freddy's case, was the best one, and so he was kitted out in a wool sweater turned inside out and a silk tie decorated with a flamingo. It was the part of his clothing that souvenir hunters had been trying to get hold of, yanking at the tip whenever he got close enough and forgetting that the thing was knotted securely around his throat.

Then, a pair of lips planted a kiss on Freddy's forearm, and a hand pinched strands of hair from his oiled head.

"Up there." Shake pointed to a platform with a microphone set before lacy iron gates. Silky ribbons were strung across these gates and tied in a flowery bow in the middle. The security men slapped away the hands and lips and hoisted Freddy up the steps. Shake had told him not to ignore the audience once he was up on stage, but he found himself turning to peer through the bars at lengths of machinery that lay over the ground like slumbering beasts. He squinted, unearthing a merry-go-round and a choo-choo train that looked just big enough to seat small children.

A clap on his shoulder spun him around. Shake bent to Freddy's ear and hissed into the coils of it, "I'll give you a cue. You've got your speech. Take this time to man up a little bit. This is last minute, but see if you can get your voice deeper."

The crowd below went wild, erupting into applause that started from a single pair of clapping hands and lifted in waves over the masses, though no one knew exactly what it was they were now cheering for. It occurred to Freddy that they were not here to see him, not really, and whether or not his voice deepened was irrelevant. One hand loosened itself from the pink mass and grappled for the ribbon. It swung when the first hand missed, allowing another hand to snatch it up before it slipped away again. More hands—child-sized and grown-up paws—sprung from the mass, to grab for that sheaf of silk until every hand was slapped away again. When the ribbon righted itself, you could see printed on the flat of the silk: Ickack Merry-Go-Gardens. There was no room to put the tagline, "A place where all is possible."

On the day the park opened, half of the state must have turned up. California weddings that June were small in attendance, the bride, groom, and guests quitting the ceremony for their cars after the second "I do"; especially hasty couples did away with the festivities altogether and simply took their vows en route to the park. Everything was trimmed with more balloons and festoonery than anything you cared to see.

Freddy's older sisters, Irene Cooke (née Novak) and Lovey Puddle (née Novak), in organdy frocks and sunhats, strutted through the crowd as if they were born into it, towing their little daughters in frothy Sunday dresses and hair bows behind them. Karen, foxy-looking and auburn haired, belonged to Irene; Patience, also auburn, and Dorothea, the only blonde in the family, belonged to Lovey. Karen and Patience looked proud of their pink frocks, the shade of blushing peaches, swirling their skirts as they walked. Dorothea, the littlest, was decked out in pea green with a lace Peter Pan collar, the floppy lapels flying into her face as her mother hurried her forward.

Freddy's nieces followed their mothers up the steps, filing behind Freddy and Shake and posing in front of their respective parents on the masking tape Xs that Shake had placed earlier that morning. They resented standing with their mothers, for the skirted dwarf-women playing the accordions didn't come to the front, and neither did the trained monkeys that carried on their heads cardboard cones from which hung wind-up models of Granddaddy that flapped their tin wings. Karen, the oldest, winked at Patience and Dorothea and put her finger to her lips. She crawled to the edge of the stage and was about to take a banana from the fruit-basket hat a dwarf woman when her mother yanked her back. Irene Cooke hissed through a grin, "Have some poise, dammit!" A photographer from *Life* captured this shot, and anyone who read the printed issue saw the pose as a loving mother fixing her impish little girl's collar.

One of the on-the-road brides near the front thought this the perfect moment to throw her bouquet. The bundle of cream and pink roses shot up and into the arms of Freddy's niece, Lovey's youngest girl Dorothea Puddle. The little girl bounced it from one hand to the other then looked up to see from where it had dropped. Her photograph also appeared in the *Life* article commemorating the park, staring at the bouquet as though she might eat it.

Shake would introduce Freddy at any moment.

Thousands of pink, moony faces, not as many children on second glance as Freddy thought there were. The little ones hammed up all the excitement that a little one would have if they were going on a summer outing, waving their hands from their fathers' shoulders, hanging from their mothers' fingers like human bait.

Their parents had caught more wind of the Ickack story, he expected, as it was closer to their generation than their kids'. But they were almost too eager for the park to open, for Freddy could see that the parents had even taken more care than needed in their own grooming—pearls and gloves for the ladies, suits and ties for the men. The parents leaned collectively toward the podium, set majestically in front of the gates. They murmured behind hands and pointed at the twenty-four-year-old paper pusher, who told himself that he *would not* dive behind his sisters and beg them quietly to drive him home.

Freddy had expected to feel something closer to pride (maybe even haughtiness) if someone ever pointed him out in a crowd, crying, "Don't you know who that is?" because he was famous. Now, there was a churning in his gut, sweat in the pits of the inside-out sweater, and he feared his lisp would return. He loosened the knot in his tie and looked out at the audience. Though he didn't smoke, he would have given his little toe for a cigarette. The world as he knew it had gone completely loopy, and he was in danger of going right along with it. The eyes from the crowd had the glazed, climactic look of people in a trance, all angled at him alone. Someone in the front row, close to the stage, reached out and stroked his pant leg.

He reasoned that this was a point at which his life could go one of two ways: He would step forward to the podium and die on the spot, or else metamorphose into another, better Freddy Novak. The first twenty-four years of it he had spent as a clown, the joke, the cartoon. He raked a hand through his dark hair, thick with pomade, gripped the collar of his sweater (inside-out and pure wool) and huffed it. Everyone, from his sisters to Shake to the moony heads in the crowd, carried some kind of fan, whether it was newspaper or a pretty thing made of silk. Shake wafted a new hat, a white linen Panama. Freddy felt himself evaporating.

There was no place at a podium for shrimpy fellows who were slow of tongue—at least, not that Freddy had ever known of.

Kicking the hand away, he thought back to last spring, when he'd watched June Allyson from behind a parked car as she came out of the Yountville post office. He'd trailed her down the sidewalk until she reached her car at the end of the street. He wasn't sure if he liked her very much; the only movie of hers he'd ever seen was *Little Women*. But that wasn't the point. He'd wanted to bond himself to her shadow because, for a moment, he believed that it outweighed flesh-and-blood Freddy, who'd never been considered for a high school superlative, let alone an Oscar.

What frightened him, more than anything, was that the people would rise up en masse, pink and gelatinous and righteous, and smother him before the eyes of the cameras and everyone in America who had a television should he deny Elijah Zallman Ickack's new place on his family tree. Lately, the pink beast was all he could call them—everyone who had heard of his imaginary, long-lost uncle, including his sisters —and now it was all melted together, lurking in his dreams, and always the same dream. Many a night before the park's opening, Freddy had bolted from bed in a cold sweat.

In the nightmare, he was walking with June Allyson down the same street, telling her about his long-lost uncle and his theme park, until she took his hand to turn a corner. He looked down, his own clothes replaced by a hoop dress and an apron, and June Allyson called, "Come on! Jo March, do you hear me? Come on!" The sidewalk had dropped off into a pit, from which a rollercoaster carted skeletons, some whole, some without a skull or hands. The cart dumped the bones at Freddy's feet—the clatter summoned it, the sound of something wet and greedy dragging itself to look its next meal in the face. It rose up and Freddy couldn't run. One million seething faces unhinging their jaws from a mound of flesh that sweated and burbled. He always woke before June Allyson could throw him in.

He couldn't lie.

When he confessed all of this to Arnold Shake, Shake told him calmly that June Allyson wasn't the name on the actress's birth certificate. "So, Miss Allyson, or whoever she is, is too proud to sign a napkin with her real name. I'd hazard she's more worse for wear than you—you're Freddy Novak, you'll always *be* Freddy Novak. Ickack is really just a bit more...*chutzpah* to your character. You could say by now that he's got pretty deep under your skin. Is it possible to believe anymore that he's only a fairy tale? Think of him as...well, as just another layer of Freddy Novak. None of those Hollywood types could say the same for themselves."

And here he was now, on the edge of the pit where the pink beast waited, and it would be Arnold Shake, not the movie starlet, who would throw him in.

chapter 2

It was a brilliant idea. *Wasn't it?*

Arnold Shake didn't normally believe in doubt, but now, he found himself listening to *Wasn't it?* falling in after the brilliant idea. He stood at the head of a conference table, where he should have been able to look down the nose at his company of one man, seated as he was. The man was Elgin Teagarden, Lord and President of Teagarden Toys. Teagarden had the type of visage that fooled clients and competitors: He had all the cheery components that equate to Santa Claus, the twinkle in his eye, the snowy beard, the bowl-full-of-jelly-belly encased in a crisp linen suit. Yet, Teagarden somehow managed to look down at Shake, and he felt the floor growing closer and the tabletop farther away. Shake told himself that it was only the seated man's good suit that made him do that, as the moneyed crowd always did to small businesses.

From the edges of the room came a papery scuttling. The accounting clerk, a little tick named Freddy Novak, was trying to file invoices, water the African violets, and look innocuous. Teagarden would cast an eye Novak's way, as though the young man were a nice butterfly that he could catch and pin to a collection board. He paused Shake's spiel to offer Freddy a sherbet candy, something new that Teagarden Toys would be releasing that Halloween. Freddy spilled half of the sherbet over the carpet, not realizing that he was supposed to suck it through the licorice straw.

Shake slapped his hands together, shooing Freddy and summoning a secretary with a vacuum.

The felt Stetson hat was a very popular thing to wear among the up-and-coming men of the year, 1959. Teagarden had taken his own hat off when he came into the office. Shake felt the emptiness on his head as though he had been scalped; his own hat was a wool porkpie that once had three red feathers in the sweatband. Now, it was missing two. He'd bought it five years ago and it showed. Everyone wore hats. Everyone who mattered wore new hats.

He exhaled and stepped a little to the right, backed by a California noontime halo.

"In the last will and testament of Elijah Zallman Ickack, his final wish is to have his mother's family fortune put into a pleasure garden," said Arnold Shake, Head of Advertising of a theme park and a dead man that didn't really exist. The theme park, at least, didn't exist *yet*. The dead man would be a character, someone you could believe in as you would, say, a great-great-great grandmother: She had been in the world at one point, had a fascinating story of how she grew a new set of teeth after having the old kicked out by a mule, but there was just enough distance between the two of you that you could make Granny into anything you wanted her to be. The dead man had to have that glow.

Arnold Shake had the fictional will spread over the conference table, and he tried not to sweat as his one investor looked it over. Shake knew that Elgin Teagarden drove from his weekend ranch in a Mercedes-Benz, gleaming like a pearl to this stuffy little office in Yountville. Teagarden offered Shake one of his pink Sobranies and he chuckled like a schoolyard boy when Shake hacked through his first puff and dropped ash into his own coffee cup.

"Pleasure garden?" Teagarden pronounced it as though he were uttering a word that might or might not be profane.

The doors cracked and it was Freddy, not a secretary, armed with the vacuum. Ignoring Shake's stink eye, he stuffed the plug into the outlet and drowned the room in its asthmatic whine.

Arnold Shake leapt in, shouting over the vacuum. "What we mean by 'pleasure garden' is nothing racy—we'll say Ickack was bound to the old-world phrase for an amusement park. Novak, will you shut that thing off?

"An excerpt from the will reads as follows: I presume that someone harder of heart is reading this document, and if so, I ask him to entertain the fancies of a man that is now, very likely, on better terms than he with the Lord. I have no attorney to tell me of my foolishness or to 'remind' me of what my mother would have liked done with her money. Nedda Ickack kept it all, 4.2 million dollars cash, inside the walls of her home, the bellows of her accordion, and made at least three thousand of it into origami frogs.

"Let me explain: My old mother grew to the height of three feet and eleven inches. Only in her last years was I her ladder when her bones grew too brittle to lift her into her bed. She was a mountain goat upon the steepest slope in the Bixby hills. A small catfish was as Jonah's whale to her. She wished that everyone could shear off but a few feet of themselves to have what she knew the Lord had given her personally. When the consumption came into the canyon, the world had shrunk to the size of her bed. She was sixty-eight, I was sixteen. She complained, stir-crazy, that the world was just not big enough and added, chuckling, that she had now and then imagined herself among my childhood toys as a tiny mote that rode the spin of my rattleback top, that whirled in the spokes of my paper pinwheels. On the Kentucky-Do-Nothing, she clung to the wooden slats at the center of the puzzle and dodged collision. It was I, she said, who turned the crank."

Shake paused to suck down a little of his Sobranie. He let the smoke flare from his nostrils and, feeling like a dragon, continued:

"In the years that followed, Mother's ashes at rest in her garden, I brought my old toys from their trunk and did as she did, shrunk myself (in my mind's eye) to fit between the slats of a yo-yo; I declare that I might well have turned myself into a speck of dust for just five minutes, for there I was clutching the string, thick as a seaman's rope, in the canyon of the yo-yo. And there I was on the outside, my hand a cloud between the hills of the slats. Big Me let go. The lurch in the belly of Little Me when the string unraveled, the yo-yo rushing to the floor to crash and leaping up the string just in time...

"When hair started to grow from my ears, I went to carnivals to get a bit of that smallness and largeness. The world had shrunk, and folks had an answer for everything. Maybe my own canyon would spread out to its old size, miles around the way it used to be; these days, it's like looking out into a crack in a sidewalk.

"This is what I mean to share: Mother's eye of the world."

chapter 3

It was sappy, but wasn't that a big draw these days? You heard people playing "Theme from a Summer Place" and turning into sentimental space cadets.

Shake couldn't determine Elgin Teagarden's susceptibility to sap. Desperate, Shake looked toward Freddy, who went misty-eyed the "Big Me-Little Me" bit. But it was Teagarden who could make dreams come true. He had a way of slipping from the brink of tearful collapse to a very businesslike arching of his eyebrows. If one brow exhausted, he just lifted the other, as though the whole will were the most tiresome thing he'd experienced since his last visit to the DMV.

Shake broke the silence and asked Freddy if his job held other duties besides hanging around with his mouth open. Novak took the hint and disappeared.

Finally, Teagarden leaned back in his chair, eyes squinted, one hand playing in his beard, less Santa

Claus now and more Euripides, deep in thought. As Shake stood at the head of the table, he would have given his eyes in return for five minutes of telepathy. And then, Teagarden awoke, slapping his hands against his linen blazer.

"You might have something."

Teagarden lit another cigarette, its paper a minty green. "Have you got a face yet? You've got no other gimmicks for guests to latch onto. If you've got a face to go with this whole story, I might be willing to throw in more than my current share."

He took a five-dollar bill from between the fifties and hundreds. "When I get a face, five dollars will turn into five million."

He strode out, leaving a trail of smoke and an air that Christmas would not come this year for Arnold Shake.

As for Shake, he locked himself in a men's room stall and stuffed his fist, five dollars and all, into his mouth, growling curses around it.

In the next stall, Freddy Novak hid his feet and discovered that he was not the only one to unload more than his bowels in the men's room.

"Shitfiredamnationinyourhole!"

When Shake stepped out to the sidewalk that evening, he gained a semi-audience of ladies and gentlemen with their pets, dogs, and small children on leashes. He stamped heart-rimmed initials in the cement with both feet.

Until he reached the pharmacy, he thought he was alone. The front window display was a life-sized plaster mannequin of a pistachio, arms and legs sprouting from the shell and kicking up in a pair of tap shoes. As a cartoon, it did the routine from *Summer Stock* with Gene Kelly in the TV commercials. Shake hated it, hated it so much he couldn't even remember the company's name.

Nuts, for God's sakes.

The streetlights blinked awake. The black car gave a low purr, so he hadn't heard it amidst his shouting and stamping. It was sleek, took the lamplight to all the right curves, over the hood like a snout and the hood ornament in the cast of a tiny angel. It puttered along opposite him, taking its time, and when he stopped, it rolled and sat. He recognized it as a Rolls Royce, one of the lumpier, older models. From the driver's window, a woman's white head popped out. Her face drooped in cheesecloth layers, and she exuded an acrid perfume, as though her organs were floating inside her like pickles.

As Shake approached the window, she peeled the shell from a large pistachio nut with claw-like nails. She crunched between gleaming dentures and offered a nut to him. "Thanks," Shake chortled, "don't take candy from strangers, myself, ha-ha."

He noticed her sleeve as she pulled her arm back —brandy-colored fur that beckoned of its own will to be stroked. Was her coat ermine or mink?

"You may not know me," she said finally. "Evette Jonquil. That Jonquil, if it's of any help."

She pointed behind him to the pharmacy's front window. The plaster nut bore a plywood standard, painted extraterrestrial green: "Jonquil's Pistachios—Try our new pistachio ice cream!" Party mixes, plain, honey-roasted, chili-flavored, all around the world where people ate nuts from cocktail napkins.

She smirked. "Mister Kelly wanted to punch it out, too. It must be degrading when you've ended up with a nut as your dance partner."

Shake chortled. "Hmm, it's no Cyd Charisse."

The Jonquil woman, whether she'd read it as true or brown-nosing, was merciful. She opened the passenger-side door. "Teagarden stopped me a few blocks back—he says you're keen on the theme park business? He's a big shareholder in my nuts. We're old friends."

She pursed her lips, squinted over the thin steering wheel at a sidewalk flowerbed, where a tiny, black bird strutted among the alyssum. The bird bent to a sprig, began to tug, until he noticed the old bag's eye on him. He stared back for a moment, blinking. He bent again to scissor his sprig in a candy-corn-yellow beak, and then he fluttered away.

In the Rolls, the Jonquil woman was musing, and Shake, in a quiet way, was palpitating. He twitched when she drew a breath. She pronounced, "Do you know, I've got a spot out in the Bixby Canyon. Well, more than a spot, really. A healthy number of acres. About five hundred. I never did a thing with them."

Outside, the clouds parted. Shake basked in the glow of about five hundred acres.

Miss Jonquil smiled, a red lipstick string across her face. "What say you take a seat and tell me all about it. We'll just circle this block a few more times. Tell me all about this place, and we'll see what we can do."

At the end of the street, Freddy Novak came out of the pharmacy, carrying a bag of raisins. The air remained thick with Rolls Royce fumes, and he fanned them away as he went to sit by the alyssum beds and feed raisins to the little bird, who hopped from foot to foot. It looked Freddy full in the face before opening its beak and bleating, *"Hogwash! Hogwash! Hogwash!"*

chapter 4

959 moved through Halloween without festivity. The only employee who seemed to cling to his job was Freddy Novak; during brainstorming sessions, he would do his little thing around the discussions, his Disney-doe-eyes flapping his lashes at everything in, what Arnold Shake took to be, a cutesy sort of judgment. Freddy's doe-eyes were all he could see anymore. The little tick came into work on October 31 in costume, a red cape tied over his usual sweater and office shirt, more Little Red Riding Hood than Superman. Shake gave him the hairy eyeball from nine a.m. until lunchtime, when Freddy, finally defeated, dumped the cape in the incinerator.

And then, there was the freeway billboard, plastered with the dancing furry creatures in bowties and top hats and God knew what all, promising a New Jerusalem complete with rollercoasters. Shake drove beneath that billboard for months and wondered what the charges were for torching public advertising.

Even the little girls' doll market was ahead of him. Elgin Teagarden came into the office on a monthly visit to survey the progress and told Shake that he'd had his finger in the doll pie for the last few years, and finally, some bright spark came up with an idea that was a redhead with an hourglass figure in a green cocktail dress and the tiniest high-heeled shoes anyone had ever seen.

Freddy Novak overheard this as he watered the conference room violets. It was an odd kind of doll for a little girl to have, he thought, for it was really something that teenage boys would better appreciate. Her lips were a bright coral red, her bosom and hips sparking curiosity, not about what she would look like in the latest styles, but what she would look like without any clothing at all. She stared from the windows of toyshops and department stores with woozy eyes. His littlest niece had one. He'd tried to show her how to play with it, though he came away feeling like a pervert.

"Named it after his granddaughter," Teagarden chuckled of the doll's inventor. "Just darling."

But then one day, Arnold Shake lit upon Ickack's face in the back pages of a family photo album that his mother had given him. He shouted, "I've got him, goddamn, I've got him!" He tore the photograph from the page and hurdled down the hall of his apartment, his heels kicking up to his ass, hopping out to the curb, all the while brandishing the face of a withered old geezer in suspenders patting a sheep.

He took the photo to a developer, had it expanded to the size of a film poster, hauled it to his second-story office in Yountville, and introduced his committee to his Great-Uncle Pearl Schacherstein. Of course, the world would not know nothing of Pearl Schacherstein. Like the true name of God, anything to do with Pearl Schacherstein would be hidden, and the public would get down on their knees for Elijah Zallman Ickack. It was a catchy, safely ethnic name. Shake couldn't see what Uncle Schacherstein's parents were thinking when they called their son Pearl. "I mean, Jesus," Shake muttered, "names like that are just *destined* to be changed."

In the airless little office that overlooked a laundromat and a skeletal live oak, secretaries buzzed from desk to desk, collecting samples of what would make up Elijah Zallman Ickack. They typed up names and places and knew not to ask questions. Shake had ordered them to hunt through the local obituaries for the recently keeled-over. "Look for someone who's at least eighty," Shake said, "see if they had any living relatives and hunt them down. Lay on the sympathy when you talk to them, girls. Their dearly departed will have the opportunity to have their memory preserved for a lifetime in an American legend—with some nice hush-cash for the mourning relatives on top of it, I don't think you'll have much trouble getting some Yeses. We need real people to make the story stand on its own two feet."

They got on the phone with the people whose names they had typed up, intoning, "Good afternoon, am I speaking with Mister Theodore Dieter, son of Paul Dieter? Yes, we are sorry to hear of your loss, Mister Dieter. This is Gloria from Shake Advertising General. On behalf of Mister Shake himself, allow me to offer an opportunity to preserve your father's memory for always. It's a project, you see. A theme park, specifically…" The secretaries concluded their messages with the offering of the hush-cash, brightening the mourners and sealing the deal.

In his mind, Shake stabbed a flag into the soil of his new territory, between a Jacob's Ladder the size of the Lord's first finger and a merry-go-round. Ickack's face shone lovingly from banners as guests shrieked and laughed. Shake, in his office, smirked. He would make Elgin Teagarden eat his five dollars.

Shake worked late these days, entering a sort of hibernation by holing up in his office. Outside, the rest of the world chilled (as much as this part of California *could* chill, anyway) and darkened by four o'clock. In his office, Shake set up the poster of Great-Uncle Pearl on an easel and sat, watching the falling light over the old man's knobbly head, bird pecking at the crown. Before the room could darken completely, he switched on the desk lamp. It was an odd, modern contraption, with a spindly gooseneck and a wide shade that allowed the light to fill the room if you adjusted it properly. Shake craned it over the photo, pointing the lamp so that the light shone beneath

Uncle Pearl's chin. It gave the old man a sort of sweet, holy visage. The eyes seemed to have widened; the lashes, feathery and long, giving off the little boy twinkle that sparked with the sweet intensity of a firework.

Shake found himself staring the photograph down. For a full minute, he did not close his eyes. The old man's withers and age spots wavered and smoothed until, for a moment, he appeared decades younger.

Shake blinked. That instant featured what Freddy Novak might look like if negotiating a bird and a sheep. He sat back and stared the photo down, conjuring in the animals' place a merry-go-round, a rattleback top filled with musical screeching, Freddy Novak's doe-eyes making them turn.

A sputter flew from Shake's mouth. He clapped a hand over it before he realized that it was the beginning of a long, burbling, wet laugh; indeed, his eyes erupted into tears, his nostrils dripped. He thought of that Old Testament passage: "Surely God is in this place, and I did not know it."

Freddy Novak, the little tick. Who would have guessed? It was too perfect. Alone in his office, Shake laughed and laughed and laughed.

It was now December 21, 1959, the first day of winter. Elgin Teagarden came to the little office in Yountville sporting holly in his buttonhole and looking deceitfully jovial. He lured secretaries under mistletoe tacked over doorways and led the office in a painful chorus of "O Tannenbaum."

On this day, of all days, Shake scoured the office for Freddy Novak. "He was here a minute ago," was the answer everyone seemed to have. Freddy's doe-eyes were now the most valuable factor in this equation, and it was as though Freddy were hiding himself now to keep the entire Ickack project in the dark. Shake's missing link. Before closing the conference room doors, he gave his staff strict instructions to keep a lookout for Freddy Novak: "When you find him, make sure I get him."

Shake peeled Teagarden away from Gloria's offer of snickerdoodles and bolted the conference room door. He slapped down all that he had put together, talking of Elijah Zallman Ickack and his mother with the gusto of an evangelist bellowing to a new flock. His staff, he made sure, had done their homework, and Arnold Shake strode in before his cash cow with a list of names and locations and tacked a storyboard from one end of the office wall to the other. For the finishing touch, Shake settled the poster-sized photograph of Great-Uncle Pearl on an easel at the front of the room. Teagarden grazed over his cup of coffee and plate of Christmas cookies, cool but quietly intrigued by the spread. He pursed his lips—a good sign, Shake told himself.

And then, Teagarden cleared his throat. "Well, I've had a chance to do a little sift through your account books, Mister Shake."

"Heavens, have you, Mister Teagarden?" Shake linked his hands to make a basket, lifted the two index fingers. *This is my church, this is my steeple, open the doors, there are my people.*

"Yes. The Jonquil Pistachio Corporation has been quite generous toward this whole project," Teagarden went on. Could he hear his voice climbing high, to the notes one can only reach when awe is genuine?

"Well, Miss Evette does have a soft spot for endeavors of this kind."

"Over two million dollars! By God, that *is*—well, I must applaud you here, Shake. A negotiation of this size—*you*—(Did Teagarden have to strain so slightly on the "*you*"?) "—what spell did you cast?"

In truth, Shake couldn't have said what he'd done to sway Miss Jonquil to her checkbook. When he stepped into the Rolls Royce one month prior, he'd anticipated sordid commands, her pickled taste at the back of his tongue no matter how often he gargled. But no, the two of them were out for a drive, every day from five o'clock when he stepped out of the office until half-past six. Evette Jonquil savored the drive and, indeed, an elderly couple outran the Rolls Royce, out for a stroll at a tortoise's pace. When discussing the park's development, she made no suggestions toward expenses, plumbing, or construction, though, about this, Shake had no real worries. She waved him quiet after a few rides, and mused over an idea about this Ickack character, something that would "rein in the locals," as she put it. Her only request was that she put her name somewhere in this scheme. Not a dollar *to* her name, just her presence, woven into the park's background. Did Shake think he could do that?

Shake was immaculate this morning in a ready-made bowtie and polished penny loafers, a grey flannel suit of his own that he remembered to dry clean. He took his place next to the photo of Great-Uncle Pearl, very nearly putting an arm around it. He struck the Torah-sized storyboard with an eager finger.

"This is the Babe of the Bixby Canyon," he began. *Thwack* went the finger.

This is the Babe of the Bixby Canyon. Mister Elijah Zallman Ickack, a foundling, adoptee to hidden nobility, and heir to a fortune. Not that he ever really knew it; a man who eats humble pie is a little easier to cozy up to, out in the world or in a story. And this is what we're doing: This is a story of the kind a person wishes with everything they've got were true, regardless of how crazy it can be.

It starts in the valley, where all the mustard flowers grow and where everything that belongs in an old legend happens and stays. Crows picking at furry dead things, buzzing flies. It's a windy day, gustiest on record; is it just the wind? Is it the flap-flap of Granddaddy's wings—

"Granddaddy? Now, he's supposed to be a giant condor, correct?"

"Yes, Mister Teagarden."

"I'm looking right now at the outline: 'Granddaddy is a mutant of the animal kingdom, four-hundred pounds of brawn beneath his wings, closer to those that support aircrafts. He is possessed of a beak and talons that seem capable of shredding the meat from a buffalo, let alone a human.' I've got the photo of our man Elijah—this little bird on his head—"

"Joshy..."

"I beg your pardon?"

"It's nothing, Mister Teagarden. That little bird is inconsequential. Think of Granddaddy's role as something similar to that of a sidekick. John Bunyan and Babe the Big Blue Ox, and now, Ickack and Granddaddy."

Continuing: Baby Elijah has no name yet, nothing but the shade of mustard plants, the heat of the sun, and insects helping themselves to his sunburned skin before the vultures do. We set this day on June 21, 1890. It's Midsummer Day, and Baby Eli has been left in the canyon for almost twenty-four hours. He's yowling for the mother who dumped him there like a runty pig, but he's just a moving part of the valley floor, as far as the crows are concerned. We know that he was abandoned, thanks to a Mister Paul Dieter, pharmacist on the Main Street in the nearby town of Carmel. A real man to flesh out a fictional one, and, not to worry, his two sons have already seen a few handsome checks, and so, if asked, this whole story is about as real to them as a family fable. Now, on this night, Mister

Dieter spies a young woman in his pharmacy, asking his customer for a ride out of town. She wears a long shawl, which squirms a little, and he suspects that she's got something to hide. The pair disappears into the night before he can get a look.

"Mister Shake, wouldn't people like the idea of him being born in a wagon a little better? Or in a whorehouse?"

"No, Mister Teagarden, a foundling, he starts from nothing. And, with all due respect, how are mothers going to explain the word whorehouse to their five-year-olds?"

Moving on. Imagine this: Baby Elijah is food for the fauna, it looks like. His cries are muffled by the hot wind. He's redder than a little tomato and peeling like paint. Half of his umbilical stump has been chewed away by roaches—

"Mister Shake, you hate the idea of whorehouses, and you want to bring up umbilical stumps? Is this going for tragic or just grotesque?"

"Mister Teagarden, we're going for the kind of thing that can happen in this country—a man rises up from letting cockroaches eat his umbilical cord to the would-be entertainment hero of America."

But we have a savior. It's a midget. Little lady barely up to your hips in heeled boots. Wrinkled like a spoiled pumpkin and with flyaway hair about the same color. This is Nedda

Ickack. Townspeople call her "Nedda the Gnome." She lives in a cottage on the slope with a thatched roof, rumored by some to make a nest for old Granddaddy come nightfall. When she talks, you are wrapped in trills and rolling Rs; you look at her and your first thought is that this must be her lucky day: She's found a fresh infant to stew in her pot.

Would anyone have come to that conclusion if they knew of what lay between the floorboards and what was cached away in Miss Nedda Ickack's root cellar? Seventy million Czech koruna, or four million American dollars. Inside that grimy little shack in the Bixby Canyon, would anyone have suspected that Nedda the Gnome was Her Ladyship Natalia of the old Hapsburg dynasty? Who were the Carmel yokels to know of how Her Ladyship washed up in California from her Bohemian throne, of how her dalliance with her husband's brother sparked a fiery shootout, leaving Natalia widowed and refused by her husband's and lover's family. Her old mother commanded that she take the next ship to America. And she kept running, her share of seventy million koruna hidden in steamer trunks.

And now that Elijah Ickack is dead, I think someone in these parts should want to claim a blood tie.

"Mister Shake, who is going to claim connection to a fictional character?"

"Mister Teagarden, you doubt, but you didn't get a chance to meet our accounts assistant, Frederick Novak. Oh, he's not much to look at now, but we can tweak a few things, get rid of his lisp—I think you'll agree that his bumbly kind of charm is just what we need. Excuse me, Gloria, you haven't seen—"

Shake looked beyond the secretary's bouffant to a scuttling pair of legs beneath a column of paper. A face peeked behind it, the eyes widening within rings of girlish lashes. The person behind the paper column ran a clumsy hand over its crew cut. Shake grinned. *All mine now.*

To Freddy, he would never have guessed that the only time his employer had smiled at him meant that he was destined for the big time. Freddy assumed that he was about to be fired and thought that Shake's public announcement was some final act of cruelty. The files he bore trembled and then slithered, paper by paper, to the floor, leaving Freddy to grapple and monkey around the office for them.

Shake draped an arm over the young man's shoulders, pulling him up and ushering him into the conference room. "Freddy Novak, don't you hide behind those files, get yourself in here—yes, you, Freddy. Shake a hand. Mister Teagarden, *Elgin Teagarden,* meet Frederick Novak, twenty-three and blushing like a rose petal. Help yourself to some coffee. Freddy Novak has agreed to claim a new addition to his family tree—yes, you have, Mister Frederick. You see this little old man? Nice photo, isn't it? I see some family resemblance there, and you should, too. You might want to stick around for this meeting, pal, pull up a chair and get up to speed on your long, lost relations from the Old Country."

Nedda Ickack, or her Ladyship Natalia, is no child-eating witch. It's only natural for her to take this baby from the roaches and swaddle him in her own dress. But it's only natural for an observer out for her afternoon stroll to take some alarm. By alarm, I mean to run down the dusty path shrieking that she'll have Nedda Ickack locked away before she boils this poor child for Granddaddy's supper. This is Miss Evette Jonquil, daughter and heiress to the profitable Jonquil pistachio orchards outside of Carmel proper."

"Forgive the interruption, but I assume Miss Jonquil has her finger in this pie, Mister Shake?"

"Yes, Mister Teagarden, she does in fact have her finger in this pie. She said, I quote, that if she didn't get off the rides skid-marked and cookie-tossed, she would have us trussed up like cheesecake queens on national television. Would you believe it, she doesn't want a dollar. Sharp as a tack. Lord willing, we'll all have that kind of vigor at her age."

"Wonderful. And she called you a cheesecake queen over the phone? In writing?"

"In writing, Mister Teagarden, via telegram. We have it among the files here—ah, here we are. Her signature and everything. I've never seen a prettier John Hancock."

"...Yes, very nice penmanship. But just one thing: I see no return address. Western Union, as far as I recall, requires some form of return address. She knows where you are—you don't know where she is?"

"It does look like that, Mister Teagarden."

"She's very generous, with her fortune and her name-calling."

"Yes, you'll notice I was not the only one she called a cheesecake queen."

"Do you have any idea of her whereabouts, Mister Shake?"

"I wouldn't want to intrude on an elderly woman's privacy, Mister Teagarden."

Miss Evette Jonquil, heiress to a small American nut throne, has nearly torn the dress from Nedda Ickack's body, not to mention some hanks of hair. She shrieks at Nedda the Gnome to drop that child, and the dust kicks up around them as Miss Evette Jonquil bear-hugs the pair from behind. Nedda is lifted into the air, she presses the baby to her, both wailing like live, skinned rabbits. Nedda Ickack may be called Nedda the Gnome, but this is only a cruel nickname for a carrot-topped midget foreigner, no indication that she feeds stray children to Granddaddy the giant condor—no indication that she has anything to do with Granddaddy the giant condor, for that matter. What would trigger this kind of irrationality in a grown woman like Evette Jonquil? Guilt, could it be? If only Paul Dieter had been on the scene that day...

"The pharmacist?"

"Yes, Mister Teagarden, the pharmacist." Shake accepted a Sobranie, offered it first to Freddy, and gratefully began to suck it down when Freddy waved it away.

"Wasn't Gloria on the phone with his son a few days ago, Mister Shake?"

"Too many questions and way off topic, Freddy."

Teagarden coughed impatiently, stubbing out his pink Sobranie. "The pharmacist...Which would make Evette Jonquil—"

—Mother Jonquil, though she would never have admitted to it before she watched someone else try and take up her mantle, wrestles with guilt quite literally. For the past six months, Evette Jonquil's father, the Pistachio King, told everyone outside of the orchards that his daughter had gone visiting family in San Francisco while she carried her baby to full term in her own bedroom, exactly where she had been all along. Locked away, curtains drawn, visitors refused by the Pistachio King, no company but for that of prodding private doctors and the King himself, who threatened to have daughter and unborn grandchild painted in barbecue sauce and left on a cliff for that ancient condor Granddaddy to tear to bits and leave nothing but his feathers. She has disgraced the Pistachio King. She would be cut from the will if she kept the baby but couldn't bear the idea of leaving him at an orphanage, and so the most merciful plan was to sneak away one hot night with her baby to the Bixby Canyon where she could drop this whole mess. Nedda the Gnome is in the May Duchess's headlock

and breaks free a moment to hear a tearful confession. "Don't take away my child. Please."

"Freddy, can we get you—Gloria, could we get a box of Kleenexes in here for Mister Novak? All but one of us seem to have come down with a case of sentimental hay fever."

"Miss Jonquil agreed to this part of the story, Mister Shake?"

"She did, Mister Teagarden. Ah, thank you, Gloria. No need to dry your eyes, Mister Teagarden? Stories like this just aren't your cup of tears?"

"Am I the only one in this room who is keeping his head screwed on? Instead of sniveling over a business plan that is, in my opinion, on rocky ground? Why, Mister Shake, would a woman of Miss Jonquil's caliber agree to a false confession of abandoning her baby, let alone of nearly allowing it to roast? Giving money is one thing, but—"

"Again, Miss Jonquil did agree to it. And we don't intend to tarnish her reputation in this plan."

Evette and Nedda stare each other down, Nedda ready to run for it, Evette crouched in her laces, ready to pounce again. And then, as though their brains have shifted into motherhood gear, they look at the baby. He's quiet now, but there's something different about him, Miss Jonquil notices. What's become of his sunburn and insect gauges? The head would have mummified him by now, but here he is, tanned and smooth and—Miss Jonquil blinks away any tricks this afternoon light might play—he has grown. At Nedda the Gnome's breast, he is as fat and strong as any baby at six months, though he was born only a few days ago. Nedda says, "Look," and opens the baby's mouth where he grins four new teeth. His hair is thick but a carroty red, while Evette was sure it would grow in dark like hers. Evette is about to reach for her baby when a squawk is heard in the sky. A black dot circles the three, grows bigger before they have a chance to think, and swoops low, grazing the ladies' heads. A nub of plucked flesh snapping open and shut, chopping up Miss Jonquil's coiffure, taking a nick out of her ear, and, as it swoops up again, she makes out a spread of black wings, opening and closing like the beginning of an incantation to blot out the sun. The creature's neck is ruffed a fuzzy white under a tiny pink head that releases squawks and bellows more unholy than those of a demon's. They bolt down Miss Jonquil's spine and she knows that this is the monster to which she had so nearly fed her own child: Granddaddy, alive and well, and turning one-thousand-and-one.

Granddaddy swoops again, and Miss Jonquil shrieks at Nedda something to the tune of, "Do something, you old bag!"

Nedda rises up from where she and the baby, now squealing just under Granddaddy's thunderings, had been knocked. She hollers into the sky the Old Country gibberish of rolling Rs and trills. She covers her ears. If only Jonquil knew that this was no birdcall, but Czech.

Nedda tells Granddaddy, the Cur of All Condors, "Janko Ickack, I tore all the hairs from your head when you were a man, don't think I can't pluck out your feathers, too? Not so fierce and big under all that mess—we'll see if you've still got big bird-balls by the time I'm done with you!"

"Janko Ickack? Where is this going, Mister Shake?"
"You'll see, Mister Teagarden."

Granddaddy hovers above this shrieking little woman, astonished, maybe, at the idea of his prey talking back for a change. He settles himself in the air and, following orders, soars between the hills until he becomes a tiny dot in the sky again.

Nedda coos at her baby and says, cool as you please to a cowering Miss Jonquil, "I pretend he is my husband. Janko Ickack was no different, maybe a little tamer. It's how he got himself shot through his head by his own brother. After that, I come here, for my nerves, never to see them again. Was no real loss, though now and then I grow lonely. Him, the big bird, thinks he is the big—you say 'the big cheese,' yes? He thinks he is the big cheese, but I know how to talk to him. I see Janko, and it is almost like old times."

"You just tell him off? A horrible thing like that?" Miss Jonquil squeaks.

"Almost," Nedda says, "from so far away, bird talk sounds like my talk. Perhaps it is vice versa with him."

No sooner are those words out than the rush of Granddaddy (or Janko's) wings are heard again. As he swoops closer, the ladies clap their ears over his Old Country screech, but it is muffled this time, as though his beak were clamped shut.

Another low swoop, and the old buzzard alights upon the branch of a naked tree. He spreads his wings a moment, between two hilltops so small behind him, catching with his feathers the sun so that the ladies and child are blinded, as if by Granddaddy's rage at being compared to a mortal's deadbeat husband. His claws scrape bark from the branch, the tree sags under his weight. He rolls something over in his beak, and it clacks like a cluster of bones.

The baby strains from Nedda to touch it. Granddaddy's tiny eyes widen, he lurches for that succulent little hand, beak gaping. Before Nedda can pull he new baby away, something drops to her feet. It is a stack of wooden slats, thick strips peeled from the trunk of a tree tied together with a bit of old string. The baby paws for it and takes the topmost slat. Instead of scattering to the ground, the slat collapses, and then the one below, and the one below that, and the one below that. And yet, they remain tied together. Nedda takes the line of slats and turns it upside down, shifting the topmost slat up and down.

Miss Jonquil watches, amazed. Had this horrible beast given her baby a gift? Made with its own claws and beak?

"Does he talk, Mister Shake?"

"Does he what?"

"...Does Granddaddy talk, Mister Shake?"

"What in hell do you think this is, Novak, some kind of Disneyland? We're going for some subtlety here—this is not a goddamned Bambi frolic. If we're going to stand out in the marketplace, we're going to have to take a more...downplayed angle. Let the myth speak for itself—"

"Now, now, Mister Shake—"

"Excuse me, Mister Teagarden, but—"

"—it may not be such an unwise feature. A communication that is between baby Ely and Granddaddy, and no one else."

"Yes, the specialists call it telepathy—"

"Novak, please."

"Mister Shake, you brought the boy in here as a participant in this whole operation. Yes, well, being as he is a proclaimed great-great nephew of this carnie maverick, we might want to encourage a bit of... creative authority when he announces all of this to the public. It's a question worth thinking about. He's worked closely enough on this project to have a say in what's to be.   And you did plan on some sort of spokesman position for Frederick Novak, didn't you, Mister Shake?"

"Speak man—spokesman position—Mister Shake —"

"Take a deep breath, Freddy. And another. No, Gloria, we don't need a paper bag, Freddy can fend for himself."

"Mister Shake—it's, well, it's an honor, but—"

"It's ideal, Freddy, and you know it in the core of that Granny Smith apple of a heart you've got. You've got the advantage of youth, fresh ideas, more imagination than any one of us would know what to do with now that it's all sagged out of us. Why don't you start prepping for the Ickack family tree now, and let us in on your creative authority?"

"But I never—right now, Mister Shake?"

"Right now. Your thoughts?"

chapter 5

Freddy purpled, for he hadn't any thoughts. He supposed he had a moment or so ago, but they'd all drained out the tube of one ear. He fell back on something he often did, an ugly fight-or-flight urge that made him feel as though he could squeeze inside of himself. He mashed his lips and eyes together, for the sight of Mister Teagarden and Shake conjured up something fierce and red in both of them; he knew that if he continued to look them in the face, without speaking, they would claw him to bits, starting with his tongue.

That face! That gait! That physique! Have you ever wanted to see your name in lights?

Arnold Shake had experienced a few of Freddy's episodes in the past. Freddy was the kind of character that you didn't know what to make of: Did you find his lisp and mannerisms endearing, or did you condemn him for the weak little shit that he was? Freddy seemed untouched by all things that were supposed to build character. Shake wondered how the young man had made it this far in life without screwing his eyes shut, pretending that if he couldn't see you, you couldn't see him.

Shake excused himself and Freddy, taking the young man to sanctuary. The men's room was clean and quiet, a meditative space that could be shared at the urinals or revered in a stall. Shake opted for the urinals; Freddy might never come out if he went into a stall. He busied himself at the mirror as Freddy relieved himself.

"Well, this is only a story, isn't it? I mean, our patrons, anyone who comes to this park, are they going to take this to heart, Mister Shake?"

"They'll take what pieces they want, and everything gets a little skewed. That's how these things work, Freddy. Who knows? In ten years' time, Elijah Zallman Ickack may see through walls. Once in the park, they're locked into some idea of what made it, and that's the thing. In the meantime, the long-lost nephew must have something to say."

chapter 6

Frederick Novak repeated this narrative for the press a year and a half later, when the ribbon to the park was cut and the gates were opened. He'd allowed his hair to grow out from its crew cut, and banished his lisp after nightly sessions of speech therapy, paid for by Mister Elgin Teagarden. He exercised his tongue until it had to be chewed back into feeling; he sat at a desk in a Hickory Community College classroom, watching his tongue wag at him through a hand mirror. The therapist, a babbity little lady who smelled, not unpleasantly to Freddy, of hot dogs, kept a wary eye on the twenty-three-year-old's benefactor. Mister Teagarden perched himself in the professor's seat at the head of the room, toying with the cuffs of his shirt and presiding over the two like a rancher over a steer and a cow to be bred. The babbity therapist, though highly recommended, went underpaid for her services until Mister Teagarden's neverending checkbook. One week of sessions with

Freddy Novak bought her a lakefront cottage with its own sauna. She sweated and thanked God for lisps.

During the lessons, Teagarden sat in the corner of the room and pumped the counterfeit will into the boy while the therapist demonstrated a theatrical version of his tongue and lip exercises, rolling and flapping her own like someone possessed.

"Now, say your Ss while you read that will over, Freddy."

"Remember to bring your teeth together, let your tongue touch the roof of your mouth," the therapist intoned.

" 'I prethume—pre-zoom—that th-sssomeone harder of heart'—she th-sells sseashells by the theashore—"

"Freddy, look at how we roll the tongue like so— She sssellss sssseashellss by the ssseashore—"

" '...Only in her latht—lassst yearz was I her—consssstant...' "

Mister Shake recommended that he continue to dress as usual: sweaters worn inside out, socks mismatched. He even added a tie with pink flamingo print that clashed wonderfully with everything Freddy wore.

Freddy's mother and father lay at rest under matching headstones in Yountville's Cemetery of Eternal Rest and so were unavailable for comment. His older sisters had mixed feelings about it at first; Irene and Lovey halfheartedly said something to the effect of, "Well, I'm not so sure, for the sake of my children, is this legal, would I be compensated?" Lovey, an Adventist, wondered if she should consult with her pastor over the matter. The sisters saw things Shake's way when he offered them one thousand dollars each. Lovey cancelled her meeting with her pastor, for the Lord, she claimed, had given her a sign and she was sure that she had made the right decision.

Irene and Lovey let their families in on it and received their own copies of Arnold Shake's Great-Uncle Pearl to hang in their own homes.

Freddy's three nieces met with Mister Teagarden at his Napa estate and heard all kinds of wonderful stories about their long-lost Great-Uncle Ely as they rode fjord horses through the vineyards. Freddy, sneezing through the dust, shared a pony with his littlest niece, Dorothea. When everyone else gathered at the villa for ice cream cake, he took time to wander the estate himself, picking at the grape leaves as though he were lord of the manor. His fantasy was cut short by the clutch of a little hand and Dorothea's strangely blank plea, "We need to go home now." Her brow knitted together, on the lookout for something wicked among the grapevines. On that day, she wore the pea-green frock she would wear on the park's opening morning. She wore a sunhat with a wide and drooping brim with her hair tucked up inside it, giving her the impression of a tiny ascetic in the desert. The wind kicked up a dust devil, and when it whirled toward them down the row of grapes, Freddy gathered her up and, shielding her eyes, panted up the path to the Teagarden house.

Such a serious-minded child. His sister and her mother, Lovey, called her suspicious. Her Aunt Irene called her disturbed, and she had her reasons: A few months back, for Dorothea's birthday, Irene had gone to the trouble of finding the doll in the green cocktail dress that every girl wanted. One month into the doll's captivity, Dorothea had decided to test its mind-over-matter at a family cookout by dangling the doll by a shoelace tied around its neck over the hot grill and then laying the doll down with the hamburgers to melt into a fiery puddle. "After what that *damn doll* cost," Irene raged, "she can forget presents from me until she's old enough to vote."

Later, Freddy helped Dorothea scrape the doll's runny remains from the grill, assuring her that, "When you're old enough to vote, you can buy as many dolls as you want to torch. On your own grill, too." He wanted her to know that there were perks to growing up.

Seven months before the park was due to open, Freddy opened the door to a troupe of characters from *Life* magazine. Accompanied by Arnold Shake, they came to the house of Freddy's sister Irene in Calistoga; the comfort of a Christian, suburban home would be more appealing than Freddy's one-bedroom hole for the November 15, 1960, issue. You would have thought that Arnold Shake lived there, the way he orchestrated, even redecorated, the tract house. Irene, her husband, and two children stood to the side as Shake said that the doilies on the tables were out, as was the crucifix above the children's school photos on the living room wall.

It was a frightening thing, the suffering Christ above smiles with missing teeth. Lovey the Adventist called it a "graven image," especially now, since the photo shoot wasn't taking place in her home. Shake, without saying as much, told Irene that the crucifix would appear too Catholic for *Life*'s readers.

"It's—well, it comes off as a bit *grim*, don't you think? This isn't to say we shouldn't play up the Novak family's devotion, but the more—*graphic* aspects of the New Testament aren't really going to appeal. We can get you something simpler, just a cross, sterling silver, if you'd prefer." Irene's family kept the one that Shake ordered, sterling silver, as she preferred. The Cooke living room would take on the geometric look that was so popular. Shake took the liberty of calling up speedy deliveries from Macy's. Shake and the photographers insisted.

"The whole house, it's at least five years out of date! Mrs. Cooke, trends move quickly, and while the park may be a lasting one, home décor is not." The Welsh armoire (an antique, no less) would stand in the front window of a thrift shop later that afternoon; in its place would be a square oak hutch. One of those bookcase-room-dividers separated the living room from the dining room. The Cooke family's books were all right: Irene's book club picks, with Karen's copy of *The Cat in the Hat*; the family Bible could stay, Karen's catechism volumes could not. The television set in its carved-wood frame was tossed out, and a spanking-new oval one that stood on three legs arrived from a department store an hour later. Some pots of ivy were brought in from a florist to hang from the ceiling in macramé slings. The embroidered throw pillows on the sofa were crammed in a closet, and three satin leopard-skin ones took their place; Irene said they brought out the taupe of the sofa so nicely.

Freddy turned one of the leopard-skin pillows over in his hands. Would Ickack own a leopard-skin throw pillow? It was hard to imagine. The photographers ate up this new layout, fingering the shelves of the room-divider, adjusting the TV antennae for a jauntier look. They breathed, "Now, this *is* an improvement." Shake scuttled around the edges of the room, setting Ickack artifacts in their places. Great-Uncle Pearl's photograph had a place of honor by the new silver cross, as did a gold pillbox with, to Freddy's horror, a hank of wispy, grey hair in it. It was supposed to be Nedda's. Another pillbox materialized on the coffee table holding a stack of magazines in place; it was full of yellowed, elderly teeth. Freddy didn't want to imagine how Shake had gotten them. Aside from these things, his sister's living room could have come out of an ad in the Sears catalogue.

He asked Shake, "Is this the right look?"

"What do you mean?"

"It's just that—we're Ickack's people, yes?"

"Flesh and blood." A corner of Shake's mouth went up.

Before Freddy could let out some of the steam that had been building in his system all morning, he was being hushed once again by a woman bearing a clipboard extracting a pen from between her ear and the edge of her impressive beehive hairdo. She wore a skirt suit a shade of pink that made you think of strawberry milkshakes, neutralized with a green scarf tied around her neck. Freddy had never seen anyone move in heels so high with her speed, and he stared until she *ahem*-ed sharply in his direction. She gassed the Cooke family and Freddy with a perfume that smelled of violets, leaning in and clasping hands as she introduced herself as Stacey Epstein. Freddy suspected Shake had hired her because of her name, all those S sounds. He was right: By the end of the week, people had a Freddy Novak routine to delight: "Well, you thee, Mith Epthtein, thorry, may I call you Thtathee?" They delivered it with reverence like comedians impersonating Humphrey Bogart. No one seemed to realize that this was the extent of Freddy's dialogue, for Shake took up where the younger man trailed off. A hint of a sweat, one missed breath, and Shake went on. He and Miss Epstein sculpted a new Freddy Novak, one with grit, a spine, things that men were made of. Freddy sat to the side and couldn't help but like this version of himself. This Freddy wore a pink flamingo tie and didn't care what anyone else thought of it. He chewed people's ears off with all sorts of magnificent fancies. But it was Shake who sat, his ankle jauntily perched on his knee, his hands folded across his chest, as though it were the most comfortable thing in the world to have some nosy-parker woman dig into your intimacies.

"Mister Novak, has this will of your Uncle Ely's been something the family's been in on for all these generations, or did it come as a shock when you heard about this big plan?"

"Ah, there was always, always a, well, in years passed, Thtathey, thorry, Mith, Misss Epstein—k"

"He gets a little tongue-tied, Miss Epstein. Have I introduced myself? We spoke on the phone this week. Arnold Shake, Mister Novak's manager. He and I have conversed this whole topic to exhaustion, ha-ha. But I'll relay what he's told me right now, if I have the big man's permission. Yes? Right, well, as it happened, the Novak family had the will in their possession for some years. It was really just a question of when the time would be ripe to bring it to anyone's attention. Freddy had been working for me, doing some minor accounting at the agency, and he brought in this old sheaf of paper—not even paper. I would've called it parchment, and it looked ready to crumble away if I went and touched it.

"I had some reservations about it at the start. I said, 'Well, it'd be fantastic, but our jurisdiction is Napa County and no further. With a project this big, you'd have to go down to Los Angeles.' You wouldn't know it to look at him now, but he's got a fighter streak in him. Freddy got right up and said, 'The Novak family happens to be the brain trust of Uncle Ely's fortune. I've got the money, and I want your agency to spread the word.' Now, take that, Miss Epstein, and add to it my surprise when this guy here told me that his family inherited *four million* dollars. Just imagine that."

"Oh, I certainly am, I certainly am. And Freddy, it looks as though you're in the shock-phase of this experience."

"Freddy's had quite a ride—it's safe to say he's in the catatonic phase, ha-ha. He's proud enough to get a project started, but he's not too proud to reach out when he needs to. Do you know, he approached the mother of his great-uncle, Miss Evette Jonquil herself, and she's over one hundred years old? This meeting with her, I suppose, long-lost, great-great-nephew did all sorts of wonders for him. Who in around the Bixby Canyon hadn't heard of old Miss Moneybags Jonquil, and so he just struts on up to that—that manor house on the hill, no appointment, and says to the butler, 'I'm here to see my great-great-aunt. I am Freddy Novak.' No explanation, just, 'I am Freddy Novak'..."

" 'I am Freddy Novak.' Listen to that!"

"And that butler did, Miss Epstein, or I don't think we'd all be gathered together this afternoon. He was about to have a big oak door slammed in his face before Miss Jonquil herself appeared, white hair peeping out of an old fur coat. Now, from what I understand, she hasn't spoken to a soul, outside of her staff, for decades. But she knew an Ickack when she saw one. Must be those big blue eyes, ha-ha. She took him in, wouldn't let him out of her sight for a minute when she heard about her son's will."

"So, is she an Ickack somehow? When I read the whole story in—"

"She knew kin when she saw it, is what I'm saying. Freddy, you ought to be correcting me over there! Now, this sounds like something out of a fairy tale, but, you know, after everything I've gone through with our Freddy, I just have to take it all in faith. He said that when she came to the door, she'd hardly aged a day. You wouldn't know she was in her triple digits, but for that white hair knotted up on her head..."

And so the country heard all about how *the* Freddy Novak had come upon his greater heritage.

Miss Epstein would thank Arnold Shake for his time and reward Freddy at the end of the couch with a tight smile.

You had to admit, she thought, the ones who could secure the limelight didn't get to where they were by their normality. They were just strange, and those whom *Life* had thrown her couldn't get by without a chaperone of sorts. Sometimes you noticed it after a few interviews; you might have thought you'd caught Vivien Leigh on bad days, when her analyst confided that she'd be all right after shock therapy. Freddy Novak reacted to her friendliest smile with darting eyes and the fiercest blush she'd ever seen. His hand in hers was soggy.

When she addressed Freddy, it was to tell him, in a motherly way, not to interrupt Mister Shake.

Irene, Lovey, their husbands, and the children hovered nearby that day under an order to keep quiet and smile for photos. They flocked nervously by the kitchen door and summoned enough politesse to offer iced tea and salmon canapés to the wispy photographers, who said "yes" to the tea and "yes" to the canapés, provided the sisters weren't using salmon from the can. Irene told them "no," and Lovey nudged the can into the garbage without a clunk.

Afterward, the Novak family stood in perfect formation on the porch to wave Shake's entourage good night. As soon as the cars containing the photographers and Miss Epstein signaled to turn out of the neighborhood, Freddy made for Irene's bathroom. Shake had made that over, too—a fluffy beige cover on the toilet seat, jewel-like soap at the sink, hand towels monogrammed with the letter I. "For Ickack," Freddy imagined Shake saying with a grin.

Freddy ran the faucet and, when he was sure that Irene had turned on the TV set, took one of the hand towels and howled into it.

chapter 8

He would have given anything for that hand towel now.

The ribbon swayed.

November 1960 made way, at last, for June 1961.

The crowds erupted: Applause like the crashing of waves and cameras exhausted themselves to get every step that Freddy took, from his spot on stage left to the podium.

Arnold Shake had a speech all set for Freddy. He stuffed the pages into his former clerk's fist as he took to the stage.

Freddy, blushing grey from television screens and newspapers across the country, said:

I never met Elijah Ickack. But I have a notion that he was a snappy dresser—I should know, I inherited this tie.

Unfortunately, in addition to a single photograph and a few tokens, it's really all the younger Ickack generations have of him. Uncley Ely, as we called him, was a campfire story who tamed a giant condor, the one we all know as Granddaddy in these parts. He was what all us kids begged to hear about. Uncle Ely wasn't the favorite uncle who gave them candy behind Mom and Pop's backs—it was another kind of gift, one that Elijah Ickack was able to pass on to the younger generation that he never got to see: To make the whole world a playground. He used to say to Mom, "As you get bigger, the world gets smaller, don't you find?" They thought it was a rather strange thing to say.

The audience—the grownups at least—nodded in sympathy, some a little teary-eyed.

But, as they reached those difficult years, when out-doing and out-prettying their own friends with having more dates or flatter stomachs seemed to draw some close borders, Uncley Ely always followed it up with, "But you girls do know that it doesn't have to be that way. There's something more out there, something that you've passed by without a second glance, that you've yet to discover. This old world is full of little things like that—that's really what makes it and keeps it bigger, at least for me."

Freddy blushed. He paused, expecting a flurry of rotten tomatoes and a chorus of "Hogwash! Hogwash! Hogwash!" from the crowd. But none came. They were all nodding, some weeping, touching the place over their hearts where Freddy and Shake's hogwash had struck.

Freddy got comfortable, almost smug.

You've heard of the kind of fortune that went into making the fabulous park that we are about to enter—you might also be asking yourselves, "What about his family? Why didn't they see any of it? What man with that kind of money would horde it all away for some pipe dream?"

Shake had told Freddy that hand gestures, big waving ones especially, made the speech more tangible, like something velvety that the speaker could pull from the air and give to the crowd to pet.

Maybe he knew. Maybe he knew that his time had come—for his and Nedda's world to emerge, and for Uncley Ely to quietly take his leave. I'm sure it would have been the way he'd wanted it; he'd always thought of himself as too big—I'm sure you've heard what a giant he was. His love, that granny smith apple of a heart (to borrow Arnold Shake's phrase) was more than, well, certainly any pie could contain, ha-ha-ha.

But I can't keep you all in suspense much longer. You didn't come out all this way to sweat in some old parking lot.

What say you, Arnold? Shall we give 'em what they came for?

If Mister Shake was Arnold now, Freddy thought, would Freddy become Fred or Mister Novak, a grown up at last?

Capitol, capitol, capitol idea, Freddy! Ladies and gentlemen, boys and girls, it is our great pleasure to give you back that cozy oyster, home again, home again, jiggety-jig, that world you saw as though for the first time. We give you the Ickack Pleasure Gardens!

chapter 9

The *snip* of scissors through that ribbon was, momentarily, the only sound in the world. Ears perked to the last wave of the crowd, spilled over into the freeway. And then, the great surge forward, everyone dashing ahead, the stomp and scrape of feet so loud the *creak* of the gates went unheard.

The Novak family entered first. Freddy dashed in to avoid the stampede and ducked behind a bench. He planned to come out once the guests had filed in and he could move among them unnoticed.

"Un-cle Frehhhh-deeee! He was just here, Mama!"

"Un-cle FREHHHH-DEEEEEEEEEE!" Lovey's oldest girl, Patience, stood on the bench, hollering until a mote of dust caused Freddy to sneeze. "UN-CLE FREHHH—Uncle Freddy? I FOUND HIM, HE'S HERE!"

Meek Uncle Freddy rose to his knees, his nine-year-old niece peering down at him from her perch on the bench's seat. Irene and Lovey scoffed and rolled their eyes—typical Freddy, always hiding. The other girls let go of their mothers and circled him. Dorothea, Patience, and Karen, a ring of wide eyes, a line of thin mouths, too serious for their ages. Freddy took in each face, expecting—what? An accusation? A tantrum?

He had always hoped that his nieces would have more smarts, not to mention more heart, than their dim-bulb mothers. The older ones, Karen at eleven and Patience at nine, were starting to get his sisters' sour looks. Dorothea would be the no-nonsense one, in comparison to her sister Patience's snottiness. Karen was an only child and played the princess with a sneer that made Freddy want to slap her. The rottenness of all this turned his face green.

Then the girls' voices burst, one question over another.

"Are you going to puke, Uncle Freddy?"

"You can't get sick now! You haven't seen *anything* yet!"

"Aunt Lovey told us not to talk too much about it before, but—"

"Oh, Dorrie, who *cares*! Mister Teagarden said we could do anything we wanted. We don't have to wait in line or anything!"

"Take us around, Uncle Freddy! I want to win a big alligator—"

And it was true, Freddy realized: He hadn't seen anything yet. He stepped out from behind the bench and felt immediately smaller and safer than he'd been in ages.

All before him was his boyhood toy chest, laughably maximized so that all its cracks and screws were visible. He'd always been curious as to how a Kentucky-do-Nothing worked; here it was, fifteen feet tall with a tail of two hundred people waiting and wondering the same thing. It must have looked marvelous from above: a great wooden square, divided by two indentations running down and across, with a crank the size of a cherry picker looming at the heart of this contraption. A chorus of squeals took their cue as the crank turned slowly, and then, with the vigor of a great, beefy hand. As Ickack had said in his will, the guests (ten to a single row of seats) flew past each other, one row across, the other down the middle, barely grazing past the heart-stopping moment of sure collision when they touched the heart of the ride. The guests tottered out, dazed and perspiring, but eagerly pushing for a place in line again.

The Jacob's Ladder the Size of the Lord's Finger: Everyone on Shake's committee—the architects, the designers, the contractors—described this ride as such, and no other name for it would do. It was a stack of slats painted a pattern of green and circus yellow that could have taken up the same space as a NASA launch pad. The guests' legs dangled like a fringe from either side of the topmost slat. Freddy had his doubts as to how the park architects would pull this one off;

the wooden puzzle was a physical enigma in itself—how could anyone duplicate the illusion of one slat falling down the pile for (let's see, how many people?) at least fifty guests strapped in for the ride? The pile dropped. A great shriek went up, along with the men's ties, the girls' petticoats, and a few hats that blew away. Instead of the crash Freddy expected, the row of guests on the top slat toppled in time with the ones below, as though it had been one slat all along that fell, and dropped the guests off peacefully at the bottom. As the first crowd undid their seatbelts and turned to go, they gave the Jacob's Ladder ride one last look up and down, wondering how they hadn't gone from the top without splattering all over the bottom.

Everyone on the scarier rides was rewarded for their bravery by a dwarf woman with a nest of hair filled with little toy bluebirds that tweeted like the real thing woven over her head.

There were rewards for the tamer rides, too, which looked like just as much of an adventure. It all must have been made from plaster and cement, and the funicular was supported by wire somewhere, but everyone wanted to believe that they were being carried in an upside-down umbrella. The smaller children waved goodbye from tiny railroad cars to their mothers for a ten-minute journey through a sage brush scene; trained prairie dogs and jackrabbits came out from burrows in the dust to take the animal treats, provided by the conductor, from the little passengers.

Signs pointed from all directions the way to the Condor's Lair, an amphitheater where a toothy forest ranger, Ranger Dale, minced through his lecture on the thirty-eight-pound California Condor perched sedately behind him. Its wingspan was ten-and-a-half feet, its wings fringed and sharp, folded atop brawn that had been cheated out of sheep and deer, fattened on zoo mouse meat. It cocked a naked head, then tucked it under its wing as though ashamed of it.

Freddy and his young brood wove through the crowds, trailing the end of a chain linked by small, sticky hands with Dorothea at the lead. The crowds parted for them, and it was, Freddy noticed, a different kind of admiration, not unlike the way Freddy felt the day he trailed June Allyson to her car. Of this kind came the cue to assure him comfort and allow the crowd a better look at him as he passed. There was chitchat and laughter that softened to whispers: "That's Freddy Novak! Do you see him there? Freddy Novak!" All grown men and women, tearing their children away from their fried dough and snow cones to point him out. The nieces saw nothing ahead but the horizon, where games and rides beckoned.

Freddy called to Dorothea at the front of the line, "What would you like to do first, punkin?"

A lispy squeak went through translations into things that Patience and Karen wanted to do.

"They've got a real live condor like Granddaddy, and she told me that's what she very mostly wanted to see—"

"One thing I know for sure she wants to do is get her palm read by one of the dwarf ladies—"

Dorothea wasn't about to let this game of follow-the-leader go awry. She marched to the rear, where her Uncle Freddy stood, and pointed out to him, because he'd asked her, the thing she would like to do first.

"You want your picture taken?" Freddy asked. "That's what you want to do?"

The others made noises to the note of "It's not fair!" But there, under a pink and green tent, a photographer squatted behind an elderly camera with a bum leg, so that it leaned forward on the two in front. Its handler looked out of place in color, a humpbacked man whose beard and moustache furred his head like tiny orange barbs.

Freddy handed the humpbacked man thirty cents and led Dorothea to the backdrop, a color photo of the Bixby Canyon. He waved from the tent to the pacing and sighing Patience and Karen and, after paying the photographer another fifty cents to try and herd them into the picture, gave up. The first step he took toward them sent them diving, terrified, into a cluster of azalea bushes.

Two pairs of eyes peered from the leaves. The humpback had turned, grunting back to the camera, and Uncle Freddy was digging change from his pockets. Only Dorothea watched, but as they hadn't thought to ask her to come, too, it didn't matter if she saw them just stroll off. Karen and Patience crept from the bushes. Patience turned back to her sister a moment to put her finger to her lips with her free hand while Karen tugged at the other.

And so, Freddy and his youngest niece posed alone on a plaster boulder with Dorothea balanced on Freddy's knees. The little humpback did what he could to ease a smile out of the little girl, flicking a hand in the air, warbling a verse from "The Good Ship Lollipop."

chapter 10

Dorothea was too frightened to look the furry little photographer in the face, but she prided herself for not hiding as the older ones had.

She liked to give herself little exercises like this to make sure she could bear the scary things without flinching. It was why she leafed through the issues of *True Crime* at the drugstore. Now that she could read (read so well that Mother liked to show her off to company by making her recite long poems), she understood what had happened to those beat-up, tied-up, trussed-up people. Kids, too. She went to the dictionary for the alien words: "homicidal," "forgery," "arsonist." She told her mother she was on a hunt for the word "providential" and was the golden girl for the rest of the day.

Aside from that, her mother didn't know how else to treat her. If Mother knew what Dorothea knew, what she found in her saintly bookworm pose, she might take them all away, every book in the house, and then there would be nothing for Dorothea to do but disappear. She got the idea that her mother pretended she wasn't there when she wasn't reading or reciting.

Around her, the rides and those who rode them howled, the sound cracking across her brain.

Why did people do this, go to a place where everyone crammed together in a fenced-in dustbowl that smelled of dead animals, to climb into machines that whirled people into space and let them out only to fill trashcans with puke. And then, people who swallowed fire or wore nothing but their own hair encouraged you to get a closer look at them. They wheedled you in with promises of palm reading, lumps-in-your-head-reading. They balanced it out by telling you of a beautiful future. Despite her Lord and Savior, Mother always went to the weird folk for a palm reading and her older sister always asked, timidly, to have her palm read, too. It was how Patience knew she would live in a houseboat, moored to her own island.

Dorothea stared into the lens, nibbling her forefinger, watching the camera watch her. The lens went in and out, extending all the way until she could see her own reflection, round and hazy, too close, in the glass. The hairy photographer went on singing, shifting the camera's mechanisms with long fingers that made a *crick-cruck* sound when they flexed.

Her throat tightened. She shifted her memory to the afternoon at the Teagarden ranch. There she was, huddled against Uncle Freddy on the last fjord horse in the line, going down a dusty trail, Mister Teagarden clopping in front of them, then Patience and Karen trotting ahead, their horses butter colored and spotted grey. They had been riding for an hour, maybe, and every so often, Mister Teagarden would drop his reins to flex his hands. *Crick-cruck,* went his knuckles. "Darned arthritis," he laughed, "you take my advice, young ladies, do your best not to get old and rusty."

Crick-cruck. Crick-cruck.

She didn't like the way Mister Teagarden sized them all up. "Sized them all up" was her mother's phrase when she spotted men sitting alone on park benches and watching kids on the playground. Somehow, her mother knew that they weren't fathers out for an afternoon with the little ones. They were men who made kids go missing; sometimes the kids turned up and never wanted to go to sleep alone again for fear of the man coming back. Her mother could spot men like that a mile away, so she said. "Look at that character, sizing them all up."

At the Teagarden estate she was, for once, thankful to be overlooked. So big, so hairy in his linen suits.

There was an article in *True Crime* about two little boys who were snatched up from a New Jersey supermarket one day and sold to a family in Oklahoma to be their little boys forever. The family gave the boys new names and punished them if they said that they wanted to go home. "This is your home now," Dorothea imagined a shadowy figure, full of fur, snarling, "and don't you forget it."

All those times when people doted on Karen and Patience, their auburn hair that curled, and said how they wanted to take the girls home with them...

Dorothea's cousin and her sister had gone from the azaleas—she had seen them dart off when Uncle Freddy turned his head to sneeze. Karen and Patience, their hair newly curled and in their pink silk Easter dresses, had laced fingers and ducked into the crowd. Dorothea saw their curls bob in the holes between grown-ups' legs, and then they were gone. Mister Teagarden being somewhere near made her squirm.

She sniffled. The camera lens coiled back, the photographer droned on and readied the flash.

chapter 11

Dorothea arranged her face into a smile. Uncle Freddy sighed and showed his teeth. The lens blinked once, filling Dorothea's and Freddy's heads with a burst of light. When their sight returned, the humpback dropped a copy of their photograph in Freddy's lap, saying, "I can take you another picture, if you're not wild about this one. It'll be another thirty cents."

In the photo, Freddy had shifted under his niece's weight and a hump in the plaster boulder that had been nudging his tailbone. Dorothea's blonde hair showed up grey—whipping into her face, some caught in her mouth. Her gaze seemed trained beyond the camera, for she had seen, or thought she'd seen, Patience, far off by the merry-go-round. Patience in shadow, holding a furry hand, but Dorothea might have been mistaken.

"I dunno, Dorrie. D'you call that a glamour shot?" Uncle Freddy showed her the snapshot.

Dorothea chewed her thumbnail.

"Hmm, guess not." Gently, he pulled her hand away and wiped the wet finger with his hankie. "Do you want to take another one?"

She shook her head. "Tish. She went off." Her sister hated it when Dorothea used the old baby name, but now it was comforting. Maybe it would make her come back.

"Tish? Oh, oh, Patience, yeah. Where is—where'd they go?" Uncle Freddy scanned the azalea bushes and the lines for nearby rides that snaked into the rest of the crowd. Thousands of sticky kid faces and not one of them looked like a Novak. He picked up Dorothea. "Where, oh where, did they go?"

They left the humpback's tent and stepped back into a crowd that parted for them.

Ladies with their young children approached him and started blathering before he could ask them if they'd seen his missing kids. It didn't occur to these ladies that the park, or any theme park, were a part of the rest of the world. Missing kids didn't quite fit into the idea—no one really went "missing" in a theme park while the theme park was open. It was more of a daylong quest that the kids were sure to return from.

"We make it a family tradition, going to amusement places like this in the summer," one mother breathed, fanning herself with the brim of her sunhat while her little boy whined at her arm. "We went cross country to that place in Connecticut with the oldest roller coaster in America, the one that goes all around the woods —Howie, Mother is talking, take this, it's a dollar-fifty, go wait in line—We're from Punxsutawney, so I guess this whole Novak legend escaped us. I just feel like the most wonderful things could happen here, that anything-is-possible feeling. I'm sure this is going to be a milestone for our kids. Your great-uncle had a marvelous mind, just marvelous—"

On his sisters' insistence, he kept school snapshots of his nieces in his wallet. He showed them to the mothers, who stood just far enough away to graze his clothes. He shifted Dorothea so that she became a barrier between the mothers and himself.

"My youngest niece, Dorrie. Yeth—yes, it so happens that—that my nieces, not this one here, of course, but the older two—they've thnuk—ssneaked, wandered off, it seems like—I've got photos, here..."

He showed their school photos kept in his wallet, the ones his sisters sent him every Christmas. The most recent ones were not the prettiest: Patience was missing two front teeth—one on top, one on the bottom, giving her a hillbilly look; Karen had gotten a nosebleed not long before the picture was taken, and fuzzy traces of the tissue she had stuffed up her nostril showed brightly in the black-and-white shot. But they were perfect.

Freddy and Dorothea sifted through ladies and ladies, all accessorized by children. They were mothers, aunts, or saddled with a neighbor's kids for the day. Not one of them feigned nearly as much concern for the missing Novak kids as Freddy had thought they would. To their shock, the ladies patted their fidgeting charges' heads and said, "Well, there's no better place to get lost, if you ask me. I'm about ready to wander off from these little characters, myself." Their children would then snap their heads up in alarm. At this, Dorothea bit her lip; grown-ups always said things like that, as a joke, but there had to be some truth in it if they were so cool about kids disappearing.

The ladies, who had minutes before parted like peasants in the pavement for Freddy Novak, now stood at a curious distance, waiting to see what might happen next. Anything could happen, as these women all knew, in wonderful places like this.

After the tenth mother, Freddy decided to use his celebrity to his advantage. Why hadn't he thought of it before? Brows creased, teeth bared, every word about to pounce, he hissed, *"Do you know who I am?"* The women jerked their heads back, and drew a quick hand to their throats, more amused than shocked. This was a horrid truth of fame: A celebrity's temper did not matter. Freddy felt himself curdling into the kind of person who threatened to sue because his iced tea was not icy enough. He opened his mouth again, then shut it and stalked away, hauling Dorothea after him.

They were aware, suddenly, of Ickack's face around the park. They had only ever seen the one image of the foggy old man. Painted over the stucco walls of the park, printed on the umbrellas at the picnic tables—Shake had hired an artist to draw up a new image. Ickack looked decades younger. Freddy's "great-uncle" gazed down in a way that was supposed to look beatific but made Freddy feel as though Ickack were imagining what he might look like naked. Ickack's wrinkles were gone except for his crow's feet. His hair was thicker, too, and, now that he was a color illustration, a chestnut brown. They'd shrunken his nose, sleeked into a proud bridge.

If the little geezer in the photograph came through the gates, just stood in line for the Ferris wheel, would anyone have noticed?

Dorothea thought she saw two auburn heads bobbing in and out among the shallower parts of the crowd, little nodding puddles of heads their own age and younger. Just over the noise, she swore that she'd heard Patience laugh—a scraping chuckle, *huh-huh-huh*, that usually scared her and offended their mother. But it all rolled together with the screech of guests and gears of the rides.

The ride closest to them was something called The Rattleback. To Freddy, it brought to mind what Noah's ark might have looked like had God told him to craft his ship from steel. It rode the concrete sea, a shining curve that swore never to rust in forty nights of rain. The guests marched up a flight of stairs to a small door on its side. Its middle had been hollowed out and ringed around its edge with plush seats. When it turned—slowly at first, and then to a blur—it jittered, a seizure that throbbed from its rounded bottom side, sure to turn a flock of stomachs within.

You always knew at a park when someone threw up. The kids on the ride became town criers when they emerged first, as they always did. *Mom, Mom, Mom! There was this fat boy on the ride with us. He puked all down his front. You should have been there. It was awful, just awful...*

This was more or less what was announced when the first two guests came running out, a pair of girls in pink silk dresses. They leapt upon their waiting mother with the news, grinning and boastful that they had bested the ride, and not the poor fool with the tender tummy. Neither of them was a Novak, and so Freddy and Dorothea went on.

In this story, the stricken one was, in fact, a girl, not a boy, and not fat by any means, but slim. To the girls recounting their ride experience, this was a shocking detail. The little girl was quick to point the vomiter out when she emerged, trembling and pale, an arm wrapped stiffly around her middle.

chapter 12

Her occupation was the worst that anyone could think of. No guest in the park had to think of it because, unlike the wandering dwarf women, her job had no bearing on paper.

Her name was Sonia, followed by an unpronounceable last name that she'd Anglicized from its German to something delectable. She called herself Sonia Smitten. Miss Evette Jonquil had found her earlier that winter. Until then, Sonia had taken up a room at the Silverado Squatters Motel in Calistoga, lumped in a hallway with girls much like herself: young, armed with headshot portfolios and indestructible hopes of being swept away by a handsome prince in the form of a casting director. They all heard that the casting directors had second homes in the Napa Valley, cool among the vineyards. She kept to those who spoke her native German and heard chitchat in Spanish, Polish, Swedish, Czech, overlapping the diffident talk of the Japanese girls, from whom everyone else in the motel kept a polite distance. Not that it mattered, for every girl in the Silverado Squatters washed her clothes in her bathtub.

Sonia, like most of them, honed her shoplifting skills since her settlement in California, and she always slipped from supermarkets with treasures beneath her coat—raw bacon, canned tuna fish, Hershey bars. In this place, she also learned how to bring it all up in the toilet bowl and never gain an ounce.

As for Miss Evette Jonquil, she was no myth. She had been a debutante, step-daughter to an oil tycoon who, for sport, turned out an impressive pistachio orchard near the Bixby Canyon, raised llamas, and, for a short time, locked his daughter away from the world. There was the pregnancy that had to be nipped in the bud. This part of the legend came to an end and was buried under the llama barn. Evette Jonquil had no baby but a large fortune that came to her, very mysteriously, after her stepfather's death. She continued her daily life as normally as possible before the side-long glances and the clammed-up horror that made her feel more like Lizzie Borden than herself forced her to hide from the world again. She shut herself in at twenty-nine, a slim beauty with chestnut curls, and emerged shrunken, deflated, birdlike in her fur coats and enormous sunglasses. She heard, under this luxurious armor, that Evette Jonquil had poisoned the Pistachio King, made it look like a heart attack.

But years passed, and with them, so did many of the stories and even the memory of what Evette Jonquil looked like.

Now, she was an old biddy with more money than God.

In the first months of the Ickack story, not long after Arnold Shake's initial fiasco, she met him in the privacy of the 1919 Rolls Royce. Shake recognized her from the start, by her money and not her folk tale. She had never attended a theme park in her life and was intrigued by the idea that people would willingly sit in a contraption to scare the daylights out of themselves. Whether her heart's desire was to expose her stepfather's brutishness or to stave off her black widow reputation, she volunteered her part happily: She'd listened to Shake's Ickack saga with more interest than she'd thought she would. She knew that she would never scrub out that black stain that seemed to mark her in every eye that took in her Rolls, the little face in all those coats. "Would this story have any room for me?" she had asked Shake. It would complicate the plot, but people, she assured him, would be smart enough to piece it together. Better she were remembered for abandoning her child, little Elijah What's-his-name, and then coming to his rescue, giving him up to a loving home with a midget. She promised Shake that it would sell.

She had a single suggestion: She felt the rides were too soft in themselves. People responded to hearsay so readily, didn't they? Hadn't Shake noticed that guests, especially this teenage generation, piled onto those zoomerang rides if they heard about the number of people who had lost their lunch on them? Suppose the park hired someone, an actor of sorts, to do just that? There would be no maintenance for costumes, as this actor didn't need anything dry-cleaned. The park could provide changes of clothes from the Goodwill. Shake had balked at the idea; maybe the dark leather atmosphere of the Rolls was getting to him. "There is no method actor out there who would even think about it. And how would you keep this quiet? People know to join some kind of actors' union these days. Supposing something happens? They could sue!"

Not to worry, Miss Jonquil said. She knew just where to look.

The Silverado Squatters was something of a roadside attraction, the way it was set up by Highway 29; any passing motorist could watch that flock of foreigners yammering and pecking away at each other in the motel courtyard. She came upon the Silverado Squatters in her Rolls, alone at the wheel this time, after overhearing a Polish bus girl in a Calistoga restaurant mention where she lived.

It was a brown stucco box shaded by dead live oaks and—what luck—home to fifteen-or-so girls.

Miss Jonquil took a few steps closer, stalking her catch; it took her this little distance from the girls to notice a similarity in all of them: They stroked a downy fur over their arms, twisted the brittle hairs with yellowed nails and scabbed fingers. They smiled with yellowed teeth, leading one's stare from the wet pinkness of their made up eyes, the swollenness of their cheeks. She need only choose one, just one for now. She would choose the girl who didn't move as she walked toward them over the dusty forecourt. The darker ones fled first, the slant-eyed ones and the Italians and the Spaniards, then two blond girls who skipped to the side to let her pass. They went on scattering, behind closed doors or to the fringes of the forecourt, afraid that she was a government somebody-or-other hunting for immigration papers. Miss Jonquil pressed on, on to this girl, chestnut hair chopped short around the ears. She could have been herself, in a younger if not happier day. The girl didn't move; it was not of stubbornness, more out of the raw fear that a beast gives before it becomes a meal.

Miss Jonquil said only, "How many times a day do you do that?" She took the girl, Sonia's, hand, flexing the index finger, scabbed red and crusty yellow on the knuckle. As a girl, a stupid, stupid girl, she'd branded herself in the same way, and she couldn't help but notice these signs of self-imposed decay in every bright young thing. She stopped herself from remembering the tang of a lemon tart, not from its fruitiness but from bringing that glorious confection up in yellow clumps—pastry, meringue topping and all—slopped in a barrel fifteen minutes after stuffing it down. Miss Jonquil preferred to think on it as a silly teenage habit, one that you would rather not bring up.

Sonia could have pretended that her English vas nut zo good. But she absorbed body language as she absorbed the leopard coat and the amber-rimmed sunglasses like insect eyes, with her nose, the tip of her tongue, the fine hairs that made a thousand tiny erections on her arms. The old woman was too curious; Sonia sweated a little less at this, let her nose tell her what this woman in fur was all about. Miss Jonquil exuded an old but pricey perfume that wafted out from her coat in lemony clouds. Her grip on Sonia's hand was gentle in a buttery leather glove—she had no plan to grab hold of her if she tried to run away. She was waiting only for an answer.

The old woman rephrased the question: "How many times a day *can* you do that?"

Sonia led the older woman down the concrete walk, passing screen doors to the other rooms. The girls peeped out, a few of them scoffing.

Sonia kept going and unlocked the door to her little room. A corner of the screen flapped down when she held it open for Miss Jonquil. The overhead bulb in the bathroom set a less climactic scene than Sonia would have liked, but muscle-memory came in a rush: See the bowl, get the first finger in, touch the back of the throat just so. Her sandwiches, cheese and tuna, came up like that. She looked to Miss Jonquil; she'd done it so neatly no trace of spittle remained. The old woman raised her eyebrows over her insect sunglasses.

"You do this after every meal?" she said, loosening the collar of her coat (it *was* stuffy in this dark little room). She spoke slowly this time.

Sonia's lips moved, she repeated the question to herself, to make sure she understood. When she did, she answered, "Yes. Or, almost every meal."

It was good enough. Miss Jonquil said she would take her to the Ickack Pleasure Gardens in the morning and move her to somewhere more comfortable. Miss Jonquil guaranteed her a salary of thirty dollars a week and a bonus of five dollars more every time she vomited on a ride. Soon, Sonia was moved into a boarding house in Napa, clean, cozy, populated again by European girls who had found better luck in the entertainment circuit with lingerie modeling. Sonia was not, Miss Jonquil commanded, to speak of her line of work, for it could mean bad things for the park, thus worse things for her. She thought of herself as a prize, snatched up by a steel claw, dropped in a snow bank in Hamburg. She kept her mouth shut.

Sonia had heard that name before, Ickack. Such a strange name. Ickack was a man who lived right near this very spot; he'd managed to keep youthful until his last breath. He had a grand fortune hidden in the walls of a little mountain shack (it wasn't there anymore, just disappeared when he died, someone said) that he'd saved up for his family to build a new Garden of Eden—with carousels and prizes and all-you-could-eat lunches—for anyone in the world to enjoy. She had the issue of *Life* magazine about the descendents, a great-nephew and his sisters' families. She didn't (couldn't, really) read the article, just looked at the pictures. The photograph showed a young man with dark hair, heavy with oil parted on the side, stiff in a sweater turned inside-out and tie printed with flamingos. His gaze was focused somewhere off-camera, right beside him, as though the world had its dropping-off point right there at the end of the couch he was sitting on and one wrong move would send him toppling over.

There was a cross on the wall. You couldn't see it in the photo unless you squinted, but it was there, a shining blur on a far wall.

She wasn't a believer anymore, but then, she'd met many with crosses who didn't behave like believers, and it never seemed to amount to anything, unless you counted security.

She'd sworn, hadn't she, to keep God out of sight since she came to America. She'd come because she'd hoped that God wouldn't find her here. Back home, she was reminded constantly of what she, unknowingly, had done. How could she forget when, as a girl, she saw newsreels of those camp liberations, American GIs hauling away sack-like pajamas with bodies shriveling inside? If God were back home, her end would be a mass grave and she would disappear. If she couldn't fool Him, she could at least try and dodge Him for a while.

She would think, instead, of here and now.

She looked eighteen, but, in truth, was closer to thirty. She corralled her Rs, broke them in so that when she spoke, the Sudetenland growl was softened to the purr of neutral Switzerland. Even as late as 1960, she would never have told an American that she'd learned to light campfires for Der Fuhrer. The night before she left Hamburg, she lit a campfire of her own and fed it her girlhood photos. Her Bund Deutscher Madel jacket had gone to the flames years before, but the evidence of having worn it (with braided hair and good cheer) had lived long enough. Ashes to ashes, and all that. The little BDM scout went quietly, bubbled and blackened into the kindling until nothing of her was left.

chapter 13

onia's dress smelled sour. It would be ruined if she didn't scrub out the stains. She put a hand to her cheek, puffy and slightly greasy where her lipstick had smeared. She padded down the steps of The Rattleback to collect her pocketbook from the ride operator.

At the entrances of all the rides, the guests were given tickets to store their purses in numbered lockers. In the operator's offices, Sonia's things lay atop the operator's own personal effects until she came for them. She was supposed to ask the operators if they had seen a green leather pocketbook with a golden clasp, her name embroidered on one side. They would know what she meant. As this was the opening day, she wondered at how inconspicuously she could ask about a missing pocketbook, in her new Swiss accent.

She dreaded asking anything of the man who operated The Rattleback. She rounded the corner to the log cabin attached to the silver ark, took in a shaky breath before knocking.

A shuffle-shuffle-slap and the door opened to a little man, no older than Sonia, though he looked closer to sixty. His trousers and sweater hung from his shoulders, his loafers a size too large. Though it was June, he didn't break a sweat, didn't even roll up his sleeves in this heat. His name was Walter Apple. Like Sonia's, his surname was a new and wholesome word. He stared up at her, his head titled back so that his skin hung in place, but she caught glints of silver in his tight, brown curls. He was the thinnest man Sonia had ever seen outside of a sarcophagus. To remedy this, he ate all the time. He looked like one of the withered bodies from the camp liberation films, reanimated and creaking around on legs too thin to lift.

Sonia envied him, even hated him, for despite his daylong feasts with snacks in between, he remained as slim as anything. She swallowed, looking past him into the office, where there were shelves and shelves of jars—pickles and peanut butter, mostly—and more boxes of snack cakes than she had seen in a supermarket. People wondered why he didn't use his employee discount at the park concessions like everyone else. She toyed with the skin of her forearm, pinching it as she ogled at Walter's smorgasbord.

Walter crammed the rest of a Sno Ball into his mouth. Most of the time, in front of other people, he ate hastily. He smirked when he caught her eyeing his supply. He stroked away the pink sugar from around his mouth and licked it slowly, almost shyly, as though he'd been caught.

"My pocketbook. You have seen it?" she fumbled, her voice loud and jolly, "Green and leather, with—"

He nodded, shuffled to the back of the cabin to open a full-length locker where the pocketbook lay on the top shelf. On his way to the door, he took a new pair of Sno Balls, gulping down the first in his usual hurry. He glanced at the second, stopped, and then grinned at it. His teeth were white, sharp. Her nail dug into her arm's soft flesh, her forefinger and thumb gathered the skin and folded. He held that Sno Ball out to her, the marshmallow straining to show a layer of chocolate cake. "One for the road?" he asked.

She would have liked to choke him with it, smother his high, growling Rs that he didn't even bother to change.

Instead, she swiped the pocketbook from his hand and hurried away. She crossed the midway in leaps, ducked in the safety of the ladies' room.

In the empty restroom, she slipped into a stall and bolted the door. Her belly grunted behind the skin, juices sloshing. All quiet but for the *scrip-scrap* of tiny sandals outside, scuttling into a stall two doors down. A lock bolted and a toilet flushed and flushed and flushed while two hushed voices laughed and laughed and laughed. Sonia peeked under the wall as a loop of toilet paper flopped to the ground and a little hand snatched it up. She sighed. It was only kids. She didn't have to talk to anyone if she didn't want to, anyway.

Remembering her own toilet, she eased herself onto its seat. She unclasped the pocketbook and removed a white handkerchief tied into a bundle. It blossomed in her lap around four white capsules, from the antimony crystal, to be taken after her next meal and before her next ride. Walter, as requested, included a small bottle of mustard water if the capsules didn't work. It knocked between her compact mirror and lipstick, sneaky in a vial meant for perfume. She made a quick sift through the bag in case Walter had upset the inventory with his sticky fingers; he looked the sort who would. She never carried much cash, as she could get her meals here free, but you never knew.

In the compact mirror, her mascara had run down her cheeks. Two stalls down, the toilet still flushed, the little girls giggled. Who cared if they saw her? She was a guest who had, per the American vernacular, "lost her lunch on a ride." So, she unlocked the door and approached herself in the gilt-framed mirror over the sinks. Under the chopping sound of the faucet, she took her things from the handbag: her lipstick, peachy foundation, blush the color of new strawberries, pink shadow and mascara for her green eyes, her hairbrush, and a pillbox of tiny breath mints. Her dress had only suffered a few stains, blotted brown like dried blood. It proved easier to get out than she thought. Her shoes, white kitten heels, had gotten the worst of it, but there was nothing to be done about that now.

Her roommate at the boardinghouse, German like herself, said she looked like Audrey Hepburn; the girl's dialect was strange, but Sonia could understand most of what she said when she threw in the Americanism "spit and image." Sonia was the spit and image of Audrey Hepburn. She was flat-chested like Audrey, leggy like Audrey. She'd cut her hair off after she saw Audrey in *Sabrina*.

"I am a chameleon," Sonia told herself. She could be her own age, twenty-nine-and-a-half. She could be eighteen. She still had that young glow in her cheeks. She was still soft to the touch. She could fit into pretty dresses, and she would make herself fit.

She made herself up, rinsed out her mouth, and popped two breath mints. Her hair and eyes shone, and if she didn't open her mouth too often, she had a lovely smile.

It would be time for Act Two, her last of the day. After that, she had the rest of the day off to blend in as a girl having a day out.

She steered through bodies, letting her nose guide her on an aroma of fried food. The food court might have been its own village. Concession stands ringed a platform of picnic tables and animal topiary in the biergarten style. Flowers, honeysuckles climbing up trellises, set off the odors of spices and meats. Sonia was walled in by smell, no time to feel homesick, only to select what to fill her belly with before the next ride. She needed something colorful, Miss Jonquil told her, something crowd-pleasing. She cut to the front of four different stands. The vendors all told her that she could have their wears for nothing because she was so pretty. They knew who she was, and they pitied her.

Sonia gathered her meal and pushed her way to and empty picnic table. She made an inventory of her food. Four bratwursts, one big cinnamon Dutch letter on a stick with extra powdered sugar, two deep-fried pickles, one bowl of cheese curd swimming in pork gravy. She opened her mouth wide and did not so much chew as vacuum it all down. She looked up, noticed a gang of teenaged boys staring over their hamburgers. Her belly ached. She heaved herself up, she mopped her lips daintily as though she'd been nibbling on tea cakes.

The antimony pellet would go down after she'd gotten on the ride. The Jacob's Ladder was next.

And he dreamed that there was a ladder set up on the earth, and the top of it reached to Heaven; and behold, the angels of God were ascending and descending on it. And behold, the Lord stood above it and said..."Behold, I am with you and will keep you wherever you go, and will bring you back to this land; for I will not leave you until I have done that which I have spoken to you." Jacob awoke from his sleep and said, "Surely the Lord is in this place; and I did not know it."

The passage was on a bronze plaque by the ticket man, wide enough to read if you were at the tail of the line. It impressed her more than any cross on a wall. Sonia knew the passage from children's Bible study back home. It had been a favorite, for of any enlightened prophet, any disciple, Jacob struck her as the one who kept his head on his shoulders.

She'd been trying since she arrived in this country to ignore God, and here He was, pushing Himself in her face.

The sun fell on the ladder, a monument that seemed to have unfurled from an opening in the sky. The first set of riding guests toppled in their seats on one slat, followed by another. The top slat looked about to crash onto the bottom but collapsed just overhead and became part of the string of slats again. It was a bigger version of the toy, the one where the slats flipped down a row of themselves, but you were fooled into thinking that it was only the one slat that collapsed. Sonia had one when she was a girl.

The line inched forward, guests started to lump up at the back. Sonia found herself sandwiched between members of her target demographic. At ages thirteen through seventeen, the boys hollered in voices that peaked and plummeted, the girls smoothed the backs of their dresses in anticipation of the gust that would blow them high.

She sighed when the ten guests, seven boys and three girls, came staggering and chuckling out onto the pavement. Four of the boys went off in search of the next thrill while the other three lounged around a bench with the girls, their dates, probably. One of the boys started massaging a girl's shoulder. The girls pulled brushes out of their pocketbooks and ran them through their hair.

The seats were plush purple to match the color of the edge of the slat. Sonia chose the seat on the far right, so that she could aim away from the guests. They need only to see you throw up, Miss Jonquil had said, they don't need the whole experience.

The antimony pellet she cupped in her hand. She thought herself clever: she'd pretended to look for spare change when the ticket man was about to store her pocketbook, and scooped the pellet up at the last moment. She feigned a yawn and dropped it into her mouth. She would swallow it soon, but decided to keep it on her tongue a moment longer, just to savor the ride up when you looked out over at the park before the big drop. She strapped herself in. She rested her feet in the stirrups below the seats, and smiled when the ride operator came to tighten the straps.

A rush of air, a gasp from the girl beside her, and their slat lifted up the column. "Hey, Richey, I can see your house from here! Your mom might want to close those blinds!" a teenaged boy called down, joking over his tremors.

Sonia looked out over the park, the guests like dots, the carnival notes thinning to bare strains at this height, drowned out for a birdsong. The California hills rose green and yellow with live oaks. She spotted far off a flat brown patch pinstriped in green sprigs—a vineyard.

It wasn't so far up yet that she couldn't make out anyone's faces. The guests waiting for the next ride smiled up. She could see crooked teeth on one boy, the matted look in one girl's blond hair that needed a shampooing, the squinty look everyone got when they tried to beat the sun out of their eyes. The ticket man, out from his booth to stretch his legs, was picking his nose. The way the sun dappled, even on him, bathed everything in a glow that forced Sonia to squint happily. She lost all account of where she was, how she had gotten here and what her business had been. She was alone with the postcard view.

She sighed, and the pellet went down. And then the drop. The view whooshed up, up, up to crush them, and the slat stopped, just long enough to catch your breath, then plummeted down again. Sonia's neighbor shrieked, a cat-skinned-alive shriek, and fumbled for Sonia's hand, which was welded, unyielding, to the armrest. The churning in her gut relieved the ache, a boiling froth that would come up and go out, and she would have the rest of the day to herself.

Another stop. They hung, dangling over the tent tops like bait. The crowns of heads turned up to watch, there were hundreds down there alone, but in her eyes was only one. The mop of dark curls, alien-wide on that body thin enough to break. Walter had gone for a walk and found himself here, solid in his heavy sweater while everyone else was ready to melt. He could have taken his break anywhere else. He glanced up, and Sonia shut her eyes, for all the drop and the threat of crushing instilled none of the horror in just looking into his face, his sunken face. The churning became a boil, a sparking geyser up her throat. She felt the solidity of the bratwurst and Dutch letters press against her insides. They would taste of acidic pork gravy. It would be all right, it had to be all right.

Another lurch, and they went screaming down another rung, the last one before it was time to get off. Sonia's meal at the center of her throat, flecks of it whistling through her teeth, and then—

Nothing. She might have gasped, but there was no air for her to swallow. That one lurch, and the meal that she had lapped up not an hour before wedged itself just so, a bratwurst and fried dough plug. She coughed, lumped her hand into a fist, struck herself in the belly. Her nose sucked in what it could, but the world began to float together, go grey and dim.

Everything now was thin: the panoramic view a murky green line. The boys down the row looked on, puzzled at first, then red when they remembered from the Boy Scouts what to do for a choking girl, before they understood that they could do nothing strapped as they were to their seats, before their faces dimmed; they glowed, and it was rather nice, Sonia thought, like little cherubs with their fat cheeks, and her fist slackened. The girl next to her was no help, flapping her batty hands, gasping with a monopoly of air, "Godgodgod, what do we do, what do we do, make them stop the ride, make them stop the ride, godgodgod," an incantation that, would you believe it, actually worked. The descent was merciful, slow. The girl went on, the "Godgodgod" not so much a keening as an old chant that went in and out like the light of this midday.

How had they carried her out? Her arms and legs, like a corpse? She begged of any deity that would have her, *I'm not done yet, not done yet. Please don't let this be the end.*

Hot asphalt warmed her back. Something pumped on her gut, like a mechanism made to drum up and down on to her. Not to crush her, because the air was thicker, the lump was slick and good. Then, light and more air filled her, and a sudden coolness because someone could see that she wasn't done for and propped her up, wrapped themselves over her and took up where her own fists left off, pumping away until the lump was good. She could see it plainly now, a mottled ball that smelled of old meat, there in her lap. Her hands went to her belly thinking her savior was gone. But, no, there was a hand on her back, another under her elbow, and a growling accent that made her feel at once homesick and at home, "You are good now?"

Walter, big eyes blinking in their sockets. "You are good?" His face close to hers, his voice soft. This was not the Walter of earlier, not the spiteful demon here to remind her of anything she'd done and hadn't known. She gripped his hand, his fingers around hers. The sun catching his curls and cowlicks in a nimbus.

If she were Audrey Hepburn, she would have kissed him. Now, though, she allowed Walter to lead her through the crowds that parted for them, out of the gate and down the road. He brought her to a water fountain, rusting at the end of the parking lot, and told her to rinse and spit. Her mouth, full of water, pressed against his. It dribbled between their lips, and Walter continued to kiss a trail up to her forehead. Water dripped into her nose, but it didn't matter. There was no one else, just them alone in the most beautiful parking lot in the world. No one was watching, not even an eye in the sky. It was clumsy, but neither of them, suddenly, wouldn't have had it any other way, for they were none other than themselves, Sonia Grunwalder, the BDM scout, and Walter Apfelbaum, a tattooed number of Auschwitz.

"Surely, the Lord is in this place and I did not know it." Well, maybe He was, maybe He wasn't. Neither of them wanted to think on an eye in the sky now. Heaven was what you made it. Here it was, this black top, this fountain, and this highway that went into green pastures where there were other places, other jobs, even if it wasn't Hollywood, after all.

If it were a film, "The End" would come in big curlicues because they would live happily ever after.

chapter 14

"Hmm. Somebody hurt."

Freddy set Dorothea on her feet at the Jacob's Ladder. The park's medical team swarmed around in a white and red-crossed show while the thinnest man Freddy had ever seen, topped with Bozo the clown brown curls, wriggled his way through.

Freddy and Dorothea hadn't been there to watch the girl on the ride and the thin man and would never have guessed that the tragedy had become a rescue, then a romance. Dorothea had only seen the body removed from the seat and toted by wrists and ankles like a sawdust dummy down the steps, so she assumed that the girl had died. She asked Uncle Freddy to make sure.

"No, no," he said, a little absently, "They wouldn't let that happen here."

"Of course not. Can't afford a lawsuit on the first day."

Freddy turned and there was Shake, ankle perched on his knee. He smoked a pink Sobranie. He tipped his linen Panama hat at them in a courtly bow, but he didn't get up. "So, everybody's enjoying themselves? Uncle Freddy's showing you the time of your life, right?" He went to pat Dorothea's hair, but drew his hand back when she flinched. She clung to the back of Uncle Freddy's sweater should he try to do it again.

Freddy didn't know it, whether it was the primal instinct to protect the pack that had never kicked in for his sisters, the awful knowledge that Shake *would* let someone die in here if he could get away with it, or the idea that Shake could sell the world this new model of Freddy Novak that would be worth nothing but cartoons in the long run, but he felt himself grow hot, and it emboldened him enough to say, "How would you like to know what I've been up to? All day?"

He didn't tack on a "sir" or a "Mister Shake." He was out of his wits. It was now a quarter to five. His sisters had been lounging in the biergarten and sipping pink lemonades when he told them. His heart sank when they proved his suspicions of their cold-heartedness: They waved him away. Irene scoffed, "For Chrissakes—'scuse me, Lovey—Freddy, they can fend for themselves."

"It's what park security is for," Lovey added, donning a wide pair of smoked-amber sunglasses, "and they get paid by the hour to do it. Take Dorrie and go—win her a balloon animal or something." After all their talk of how they would *never* let their children out of sight in places like this...

"So, would you?" Freddy hissed at Shake. "If you don't want to worry about a lawsuit on the first day." Back straight, arms crossing the chest.

Shake blinked. Freddy, threatening? Even if it was a poor threat, this was new. "Well, I'm agog to learn. Tell me about it."

"I've been circling around and around this place to look for two children, two little girls, that somehow your security doesn't seem to feel even a mote of responsibility for."

He glanced up: The funiculars teetered across the park, little flying arcs in the sky. It was where he'd met one out of the many guards of park security, and Freddy might have missed him entirely, for his candy-colored golf trousers and linen shirt suggested the visage of a merry civilian. He hid his officer's attitude well behind a pair of sunglasses. They were all meant to, and it was rather good idea, having undercover guys.

Freddy and Dorothea had gone down the line of guests waiting at the funicular entrance, pushing every gap-toothed grinning photo into their faces, Freddy chanting their names and Dorothea their ages like a rosary: "This is my niece Karen, she's eleven. This is my niece Patience, she's nine. Karen is four foot ten, Patience is four foot eight. They've been missing since we got into the park." He stopped

Freddy, lowered the sunglasses like insect eyes and nodded. It didn't make him look like more of a person, Freddy thought, though his eyes were blue. The merry insect stepped out of line; he had a golden badge the same color as his hair and told him, *sotto voce*, "You've got guys like me here to make sure no one makes off with the big bird—"

"It's a condor," Dorothea murmured. The insect man chuckled but kept his hands in his pockets. She'd snap his fingers right off if he went to pat her on the head.

"But it's things along those lines, big bird heists, that we're really around for. Now, I'll take a look at these snapshots—mmmhmm, hmmm—I'll keep an eye out for you, but it's really not worth the worry. The ticket guys can see how tall they are, so your kids can't sneak on the Rattleback if that's what you're worried about. How old are they—ten, eleven? Right, so don't put it past them to navigate their way around. Meantime, you take your little girl to see that great, big condor."

It went on like that, badges and insect eyes in outing clothes. They liked to hover at the edges of the crowds and buzz their way in as soon as Freddy flashed the six photos and sounded the alarm. You would think that kids with their names in the papers would hit a public nerve if they so much as stepped in fresh dog turd. And he knew as well as any tabloid-hound that a celebrity's misfortune was a civilian's merriment, whether it was Haley Mills stepping in dog turd or Rosemary Kennedy's lobotomy.

It was infuriating. Why didn't Freddy just let it go? It was hardly the time to admit it, but Freddy Novak would have been content to disappear at ten or eleven, let alone take a day's wander. Might there have been, however, someone up there who liked him, someone to watch over him should he find wicked things when he was on his own? No one carried a snapshot of Freddy Novak when he was *only* Freddy Novak, slow of tongue and buzz-cut. If the wander turned into a vanishing, would anyone have tried to conjure him back? Mom and Dad, rest them, were the type of people who swallowed the urge to introduce him to strangers as the neighbor's boy; his sisters had been his reluctant keepers. And behold, their mothering instincts had not improved with their own children.

There were scads more of them in the park, these mothers burdened by their offspring. It made him rub the school photos in the faces of the guests, mainly ladies. Rub them in good and rough. "You've barely *looked* at this damn picture, don't tell me you haven't seen them if you don't even know what color their hair is!" And—*pop!*—there they were, a pair of shiny black eyes and a strong arm to pull him aside, telling him to settle down. The park security had a way of talking that always began with, "Now, son..." This, with the plainclothes, was supposed to put you at ease. To Freddy, it paved the way for more instances of being talked down to than he'd ever experienced in one afternoon. The guards took him to benches or picnic tables, tried to garner a little trust by rewarding Dorothea (for what?) with chewing gum. She glared at it until the guard stuck it back in his pocket. Freddy envied her—look at that face, the little disdainful snarl that no one seems to know how to use until their teens, on a freckly child's head. Freddy could learn something from her. He sat through five different insect men placating him with the same reassurance that his kids were just fine. "Look, I know who you folks are. We don't want any trouble. So before you bring out the attorney arsenal, might I suggest you sit down here for a spell, keep your eyes peeled—"

While the guard had launched into his "don't worry" jargon, Dorothea had crept up behind him and sunken her teeth into the pasty white hand that offered her the chewing gum. It was wonderful, for her jaw was like that of a Rottweiler's, leaving twelve tiny marks right in the ham. She knew to play dumb, pulling on her lower lip, asking sweetly, whining, "Where did you put the bubble gum?" It was all that kept the guard from striking her. Growling over the mark on his hand (any deeper, and Dorothea would have drawn blood), he dug through his pocket and foisted a wrapped ball of gum in the little girl's face and allowed them to move along unmolested.

Freddy wasn't yet at the point of punching someone out, though he soon would be. He was reared up already. He had Shake trembling—the one leg, anyway, but it was something. "It might be my name in the park, but we both know who this place really belongs to. Teagarden promised everything, security included, and it's bizarre that everyone on his payroll lets it slide. You know how big this place is. It would not have occurred to you that two loose kids in the park, two *Ickacks* might be of interest to someone? My kids—Do you know, I've been calling them *my kids*? You wouldn't know my sisters ever had any. Does any of this sound interesting to you?"

Shake's leg bounced, his ankle still at rest on his knee. The pair of them, the paper-pusher and his mute infant sidekick, had the look of badgers ready to compete for the fattest bees' nest. He picked his words carefully: "I wouldn't say they're lost. Not alone, either."

Freddy let go Dorothea's hand to strip off his sweater. He tossed it on the bench, dropped the flamingo tie in a trashcan, and pushed up the sleeves of the white shirt underneath. He unbuttoned the collar. Stripped of layers, he took up space, and Shake felt himself drawing inward to accommodate this new Freddy Novak. Just like that, he aged a decade, no longer a child. He now looked twenty-four.

"Not lost," Freddy repeated, "not alone. With anyone I know of?"

"Mister Teagarden was kind enough to suggest a private tour with the children, and—"

"Why with him? I could've taken them around myself—"

"He *and* your sisters felt, and I agree, that it would have been claustrophobic. You have a national face. You were dive-bombed by folks as soon as you came in. Now, how would that have panned out for the kids?"

"Teagarden got the okay from my sisters?"

"You heard me, yes."

"Well, hell, why didn't they say so? It would have put a lot of awful fantasies to rest."

"Freddy, I wouldn't have put it past you to conjure up something awful, anyway."

"So, is this where Mister Teagarden comes in, playing babysitter?" Freddy chuckled.

"Freddy—*Freddy*. Just let him have them. Let him have them."

Shake took a silken handkerchief from his breast pocket, mopped his cheeks.

Just let him have them. Freddy couldn't be sure if he'd heard Shake correctly, but there it was. "And do what with them?"

The handkerchief was damp in two blots. Shake sighed, went to mop his face again. Freddy snatched it away, waved it, a green banner, for a prize before balling it up and shooting it in the trash can. "And do *what* with them?" he snapped.

Teagarden doling out speech lessons, pony rides, confections like an old gnome. Wouldn't he expect, by now, something in return?

Shake was quiet. "Anything they want to do," he said finally, his voice too high, too innocent.

From somewhere in the sky, a speaker crooned like Dion DiMucci or Paul Anka, one of those starry-eyed boy singers. Someone must have liked it very much, enough to whine again and again, "Why?"

As though this were somehow a trigger, Shake's head drooped, a weight on his neck, and he let his hand take the burden. He wiped his eyes as he spoke. "Just give Teagarden the day. The one day is all he wants, that's it. This place—none of this—" he raised an arm for Freddy to take in the screeches, the whir of the gears—"none of this is mine anymore. Teagarden Toys wrote half the checks since day one. We've got endowments coming in like you wouldn't believe. He's been in conference with chocolate corporations all over; Ickack could be a Halloween treat come October. Evette Jonquil would never have looked us in the face if he hadn't gotten to her first."

The refrain kept going, someone singing it on an infinite loop. One thing could be said for whoever it was: It had Dion DiMucci's lament down pat. "Whyyy—yyy?"

"So," Shake snuffled until his breath came fast. "What's two little ones as a thank you, from you to him? He wants to see them. Nothing else.

"Nothing else. And he's set your folks for life. They wouldn't breathe a word about it, so it's no use getting after those sisters of yours. Just one day, for—that's a small price for what it takes to send the kids to top-notch schools, like they deserve. Mingle with a better class of people. The girls, they'll be doing cotillion balls and whatnot, it's enough to make them forget. He's not above having you ruined. You interfere, you even think on it, he'll take your sisters right down the same goddamn toilet with you—"

"*Whyyy-yyy? Whyyy-yyy? Whyyy-yyy...*" A cicada picked up the harmony.

Freddy Novak imagined the cotillion balls his nieces would attend. He saw Karen and Patience as debutantes, teenaged ladies, acting out the princess fantasy that had never come to fruition in their mothers' youth in pink roses and ivory satin gowns. Though his nieces were supposed to be having the time of their lives, it would be at a cost. They stumbled on their high heels and collapsed over their long skirts. They wept, and Freddy reached to wring Shake's rooster neck when the whining song grew louder.

The singer's voice came from their nose, almost like a kazoo. It carried over Freddy's and Shake's heads as he serenaded them from the treetops. Only a kid would find this funny,

"*Whyyy-yyy? Whyyy-yyy—*"

"Will you *shut*—" Freddy spun on his heel. Behind him, a live oak, no crooning Romeo in the branches.

He made a fist, but it was sticky with the gum Dorothea hadn't chewed. *Dorothea!* She hadn't missed a word, had she? He felt for her hand.

"Dorrie?"

In a tiny shoeprint, little grooves in the dirt, a gum wrapper fluttered and drifted off.

The first place he went to was the Lost Children's Cottage. It was the first logical place he should have gone to, anyway, he thought, clapping a hand to his forehead. Leaving Shake at the bench, he threaded through bobbing heads and balloons. A flood of relief swept though him when he saw it, a little Seven Dwarfs hut of plaster and green trim and begonias in flowerboxes. The spinster nanny who answered opened the door to a room filled with plush animals, rag dolls, a cushioned infant seat, and a miniature piano. There were four little beds, made up with gingham and eyelet covers. But not a child in sight. She glanced at the photos Freddy offered and said, "They're nine and eleven, you said?"

"And six! I—I lost another one just now, her name is Dorothea Puddle. She's the younger sister and cousin of the other girls—"

"Sir, maybe you can't tell, but this is meant to be a place for very little children. And I should tell you," she added, ticking a bony finger at the wall clock, "we close up at five."

Freddy's hands curled. "So, do kids have a curfew not to go missing after five o'clock in this place?" he snorted, "What's a lost child supposed to do at five-oh-one?"

"There is no need to use that tone of—" The cottage nanny backed into the little room, her hand clamped on the door.

All at once, Freddy saw every hand on every door that had slammed in his face within an inch of cutting off his nose. Twenty-four years of doors slamming, even in his celebrity.

He wedged in his foot.

The nanny gasped, wrestling the door closed. "Sir, please, get your foot out—please, sir, I'll have to ask you to—" she heaved her weight into it, switching tactics. In a spare moment, she grabbed up the little piano, it might be a fair bludgeon, if she needed it. "Sir, I will call the authorities right now, if you do not —"

The door gave. Freddy took a step back, held up his hands. "Fine," he sneered. "Fine. That's just fine."

The cottage nanny heard his voice drop to the ground. She peeked out. Freddy Novak was settling into one of the wide flowerbeds under the window, legs folded under him, nesting in the dirt like a brooding mother bird. He picked a begonia, sniffed it, and stuck it behind one ear.

"I'm happy to wait out here," he breezed, plucking another begonia and then another. "I'll just get cozy until you decide what's going to happen next. It's all up to you, lady." He whistled idly, and then hummed, then broke into a rumbling bass voice from somewhere deep in his chest as he assembled the picked begonias into a very pretty little bouquet.

He went on like that, singing and plucking leaves and blossoms alike. He went through all the songs he could churn out: "Searchin'," "Not Fade Away," "Yes!

We Have No Bananas," "Ain't That a Shame," "That'll Be the Day." He would wait all night, latch himself here like a tick. He found that being a pest, the most aggressive sort of pest, was the way to get what you wanted. A few years later, he would find himself doing a similar thing, a sit-in at the gates of the White House, dressed in blue jeans and a headband, carrying flowers for the boys in Vietnam. His songs then would include a lot of Jefferson Airplane, sung through tear-gassed sobs. He would look back on this moment, June of 1961, as practice.

Time passed in the gliding of the sunlight, slipping lower and lower until it reached the tips of the yellow hills beyond the park, and everything was made balmy and golden. He turned, meeting the papery face of the cottage nanny through the little window.

The cottage nanny kept her post, flicking back the gingham curtains with a stubborn hand. It was not Freddy she watched for, though his presence made her toes curl. She remembered her orders from Mister Teagarden, and she was not one to cross a man who promised her a hundred shares in Teagarden Toys. "Lock up at five," he'd said, "and leave the key. I'll trust you that there will be no one else around." The cottage nanny did not ask questions, not with a hundred shares coming to her. The clock, with its face done up as a teddy bear with plump, ticking hand, struck five. She peered outside, squinting, and there, far off beyond the smoky aroma from the food court and through the trumpet flower vines, was a linen suit, luminous and round and as white as a mushroom. Mister Teagarden wore such fine suits. In his wake were two little girls, sagging from his furry hands.

Freddy's gaze was in another direction, up in the reddening clouds.

The nanny disappeared into the cottage, fumbling through the plush creatures until she reached a telephone, pink and tall in the candlestick style. She wound the number through and jammed the earpiece to the side of her head. "Yes, this is Miss Martha Bergen at the Lost Children's Cottage. I want to speak to Mister Shake...Well, where is...If he was just speaking with Mister Novak, you could certainly send someone out to find him and bring him here... Well, I've got Mister Novak here...No, I want him gone! At once!"

chapter 15

"**W**hyyy-yyy?"

Dorothea saw the little black bird before he saw her. He hopped from foot to foot on a branch in the live oak, and when he'd decided he'd had enough of that one, he'd make his way to one beneath him without as many leaves. Dorothea had never seen a bird like him: sleek, black, proud feathers he wore like a tuxedo, yellow needle of a beak, quite big for a songbird.

He cocked his head, and the boy singer's voice asked her, "*Whyyy-yyy?*"

Dorothea took a step forward—careful, now, don't scare him off. He spread his wings, not frightened, but like arms spreading to say, "*Come in, come right in.*"

He stuck his head out, down at this tiny girl pulling gum wrappers from the pockets of her yellow dress, then took off for a tree across the path. Just a dark blur, and she could see him in the lowest branch. He could have pecked at the bouffant of the lady on the bench below, but he didn't. Instead, he opened his beak and screeched into her ear, "WHYYY-YYY?" His audience jerked from a daydream, screeching,"Hoh, Jee-sus!" upsetting a mason jar of root beer float down her front. She scooped vanilla ice cream from her bosom.

Dorothea laughed, the same raucous *haw-haw-haw* of everyone who watched the lady fling bitter slops of ice cream and stomp away to the nearest restroom. But even she could crack a smile after that because everything was all right. It was only a dress and it was a lovely day.

Dorothea went on down the path. A black and yellow dot hopped from tree to tree; the bird waited for her to catch up and was off again. The sun began to sink, and the park truly had the look of a pleasure garden now. The pink gold faces of the guests matched the palate in the clouds, and everyone strolled along, hand-in-hand.

The little bird rested on the roof of a little brick hut, the restrooms, until Dorothea reached him. And then he was gone again.

She rounded the corner to the games arcade. The sound of balloons bursting made her jump. But it was only kids and their parents throwing darts for prizes. She stood in the middle of the alley, chewing a fingernail, and no one stopped to ask her where her own folks were. The kids aimed shotguns at rotating tin wolves and rows of balloons and were rewarded with big game—stuffed grizzly bears and coyotes. four feet tall. Every face was washed with green, red, orange lights. The little girls took home dolls with china faces. The dolls were large enough to be toted piggyback style, and so they trouped out that way. One little girl staggered along, weaving from foot to foot under a giantess in a green frock and leatherette booties. The doll measured four feet standing up, but its owner insisted hauling it out herself.

As they went by, the doll's tiny new mother whistled—really, grunted—her way through "The Colonel Bogey March." And, to Dorothea, every little girl and every doll was like a soldier, huffing the fallen to the Red Cross fast as they could go. Get them out of the line of fire. Shrapnel's gone too deep, right through the bloomer; we'll never clot the sawdust— we're losing her.

Dorothea eyed the skies, the spires of the games tents. No one whistled back.

She shivered. Patience taught her the dirty version of that march that they'd learned in school, and it was delicious to have that secret together. Tish had brought Dorothea far away, behind the hedges in the backyard, so their mother wouldn't hear. But how could you keep a lid on something this brilliant, a word you used all the time, and it turned out to be absolutely filthy, in the right way?

Soon, they were treating the whole neighborhood to a concert, and Mrs. Pinkerton next door stomped over to complain. It was the first time the children had ever been punished together; they went to bed without supper, but after their parents had turned in, they feasted on pretzels, chocolate chips, and marshmallows, nicked by Tish from the kitchen. A midnight feast. Dorothea heard a tiny singsong and realized that she had been singing to herself. She imagined Karen taking up the harmony, Tish on a kazoo. And then Teagarden's face, like a drooping pumpkin head, loomed over them all. He flexed his hands, *crick-cruck.*

She picked up the pace, quietly singing, "Goering has only got one ball, Hitler's are so very small..."

A little way down the alley, she could see Granddaddy. Not the real thing; it was a life-size automaton that jerked and pulsed and regurgitated prizes. A little boy stepped back to catch a rabbit's foot key ring that flew from its beak. The automaton's stall glowed with the light bulbs of the kind hairdressers fix around salon mirrors. They flashed at millisecond intervals. Dorothea rubbed her eyes. Granddaddy perched on a tree limb that sagged. His feathers were ragged; they had a matted look to them, as if they had fallen out and had to be reinserted with glue. His head, wrinkled like an old onion, bobbed with creaks. His wings spread open and closed, his body jerked with the labor of it. It looked unnatural, like a corpse that couldn't be let to rest in peace. She put out a finger to touch. Granddaddy let out a squawk, he spread his crooked wings with snaps and cracks, and he went still.

There was a curtain at the back of the stall and a man came out in a plaid shirt and jeans, finishing a cigarette. He tossed the butt in the dirt and started to fold Granddaddy's wings back into place when he noticed Dorothea. He didn't read *Life*, so she was nobody. "Sorry, hon. Robo Granddaddy's got to get his beauty sleep."

She swallowed, wiped her nose. She played along. "Does he do anything? When he's not sleeping?"

The man gave Granddaddy's head a pat. The sound was hollow, like knocking on plastic. He took a rubber mouse from his pocket. "Well, you try and feed him one of these, and if you get it in his beak he'll give you a prize. From here." He opened a door in his belly, to a cavern filled with yo-yos, miniature Jacob's Ladders, kazoos, slinkies... "Hope that didn't kill the game for you," the man said, "but you come back some other time when this guy's awake."

He took a crate and stared piling in orange hippos. He stopped, turned. She was still there, looking at the mechanical Granddaddy as though she were expecting him to awaken. "Is your mom or dad around somewhere?"

She looked up. The little black bird had come back; he hopped from one foot to the other two stalls over. "Oh, over by the food place, the beer place, whatever it is. They said I had to meet them there for supper."

"Well, it's honing in on six. You'd better get a move on. Have them get you one of those chow mein sandwiches while you're down there." He went back to packing the plush hippos.

She went down the flashing alley of Whack-a-Bear, Smack-a-Mole, Slap-a-Fish, Beat-a-Moose, trained to the black dot in the sky until it dropped, soaring in a downward arc, leading her eye straight on to a bench. A little old man sat there, peaceful in his layers of sweaters, flannel shirts and cotton trousers. The heat, going on sundown and clinging to eighty degrees, didn't touch him. On his feet were loafers, the leather filthy but the pennies in the tongue-slit fresh pink from the mint, and he gave off a rich, wonderful smell—soft earth after rain. Age spots stood out on his bare scalp, while his hair grew in a thicket from the temples down. Dorothea had only ever seen hair so unruly in pictures of storybook warlocks. He'd been mumbling, sometimes singing to himself up until now from behind his beard, white threaded with grey, his tongue flicking out to lap at the fringe of his mustache. The little black bird hovered for a moment, then dove when the little man began to whistle. And a lovely whistle it was, clear as a tin pipe and sweeter, maybe, from a missing tooth. Dorothea recognized it and burst out laughing, the first time in ages: It was "The Merry-Go-Round Broke Down."

And the little bird answered to it, settling himself on the crown of the little old man's head. Dorothea could have been the only soul for miles, though ladies, men, their children stumbled past her to avoid the derelict on the bench. Suddenly, his head jerked upward, and he uttered a very merry-sounding, *"Baaa!"* Dorothea giggled, and she remembered a line from one of the poems her mother made her recite: "I sound my barbaric *yawp*..."

She had seen him before, maybe on a curb in Yountville sipping on something from a paper bag and cursing. But somehow that couldn't be it. A step closer, and she caught (she hoped she didn't) a flicker of Mister Shake, the same way they both had of lifting their upper lips when they sniffed, like rodents. But it was gone. He reached up a finger for the little bird to nibble.

"He's a good old bird," he said in a flannel-sounding voice. "Real good bird, smart as can be. Did you know, I taught him to be a sheepherder? Well, I surely did. Fifteen of 'em, and he can get 'em all penned by six pee-em, even if there's one wandered out to Canada. Used to whistle 'Meet Me in St. Louis,' but the sheep are pretty keen on that 'Camptown Races.' "

Dorothea glanced over her shoulder. Yes, he was talking to her.

The bird nodded proudly each time he was mentioned. There had never been a better sheepherder, and he knew it. *"Doo-dah, doo-dah day,"* he squawked.

And she knew him. Her family had his picture in their house, perched on a place of honor on their mantelpiece where the children's school photos used to be. They weren't kin, though the children were supposed to tell everyone that they were.

She took a step closer. The little bird on the old man's shoulder must have wondered what it was like to be a sheep and tried out a good, *"Baa-aa."* The old man chuckled and let the bird nibble at his ear. "They got a good picture of me and him, the day I got him," the old man said, "Would you believe, Mister Joshy, this old bird, had his thirteenth birthday? Well, I don't. Best not to tell him something you want to take to the grave—can't keep a secret to save his life...And birds like him live forever. Or eighty years, whatever the Audubon books say..." He let his head droop to the side, then perked up again. "I had a nephew, you know. Name in the papers. Never thought I'd see him in the papers. For anything worth reading on, anyway."

Dorothea's eyes widened. And so, was Uncle Freddy an Ickack after all?

The old man picked a hump of callus on his thumb. "Shake, he calls himself," he mumbled.

"Where does he dig up that kind of name? Arnold Shake, how are you? The day I got old Joshua—I do believe that's the last I saw of little Arnie. His people came from out east, stuck me in a home. Or tried damn hard at it. 'Pearl,' they said, 'Pearl, your mind has gone. You come with us, we'll take you somewhere with folks that have a way with people whose minds have gone.' Set the sheep on 'em, is what I did. You wouldn't know it to look at them, but they got fangs, take a bite outta ya."

She'd seen those kinds of homes, they'd set up her Granny Puddle in one last summer. Why did everyone call it a home? The chill of the cinderblocks and the smells of old urine and pasta salad. The commode out in the open for the world to hear your waste splatter. On the outside, it had the deceptive look of a dollhouse. It was no wonder Granny Puddle used "such language" when Daddy visited.

She held out her hand. No need to be afraid here.

chapter 16

Freddy was coming up in the world. The insect men had him swarmed, just as he was finding that he could to a rather impressive Buddy Holly impersonation and had a budding talent for flower arranging. He offered the security men a nosegay as they snatched him up and hauled him out of the flowerbed.

He knew that they would not throw him out.

Shake's office, high up and hidden in a thick-trunked plaster tree, loomed over the park. The slightest breeze sent a cloud of small birds fluttering over the evening sky, all of them black in the fading light.

He let Shake bring him up into the tree's top floor, overlooking the American Condor cage. (If Freddy was going to hit him, it would save the park's reputation if he did it behind a closed door.) The better class of employees, such as Arnold Shake, looked out at the lay of the park through strings of ivy and pink trumpet flowers. The rides whirred, and the guests howled a joyful noise into the darkening sky.

Shake showed Freddy one of the leather chairs and turned to the Italian coffee pot, saying, "Miss Bergen was really quite upset when she called. She told the guards—Good Lord, I never thought you had it in you. I'm almost proud of you—you, vandalizing, public disturbance, attempted breaking and entering. She said she suspected you'd been drinking—you old ghoul. Why don't you just settle down—"

Freddy took his coffee, swirled the contents of the mug. Before he could talk himself out of it, he drew it back, hurling hot Italian bean juice in Shake's face. Shake hissed, spat coffee running like blood from his mouth. It gave Freddy the perfect chance to add that touch, his fist in Arnold Shake's teeth. Shake, still blinded from the coffee assault, tongued his bottom row. He spat again, red and stringy. "Little shit, I'm toothless!" He threw the missing incisor; it bumped off Freddy's chest with a tap.

He reared back, as if to tackle Freddy Novak, but thought the better of it. Freddy gripped the mug handle like a bludgeon.

Shake panted, "The man gave his word. And if you knew Teagarden, his word is a surefire thing. Nobody is coming away damaged—"

Freddy lunged, and Shake darted behind the great oak desk, his gold leaf nameplate spinning. Shake snatched it up, just in case.

Freddy swiped at the hand that held it. There was a *ding* when porcelain met knuckle, and the nameplate, now free, rolled far away under the radiator. He took the hand that Shake nursed, slapping it over the desktop, knocking over papers, pens, the typewriter, the African violets, until they found the telephone, black and large, used for making interoffice calls.

"Get on the phone," he hissed.

"And call who? The police are celebrity hounds, too, you know. You think it'll just keep quiet, between you and ugly?" Meaning Teagarden. "Everyone saw the kids with you when you came in. You make Teagarden into a monster, you'll get eaten alive by every mother in the nation." He tried to bring sourness into his smile, but his mouth ached.

Freddy grabbed up his other hand. He hadn't heard a thing. "Get. On. The. Phone. It's your park, too."

"Mister Shake." A tinny voice came from behind the African violets. Then Shake groped for the Bakelite box behind the flower pot—the intercom. The phone extension had been knocked from its cradle, and a female voice asked again, *"Mister Shake? Hello, Mister Shake?"*

He grappled for it. He gasped, kept his voice straight, professional. "Yes. Yes, Gloria." Freddy kept a stiff hand on the back of Shake's neck.

Shake's secretary on the tower's bottom floor paused, then went on. "Mister Shake, there have been complaints from the guests about a—ahm—a strange character in the park. He sounds like a vagrant type, but he's got a ticket stub—"

"What's he been up to?"

"Well, nothing, really. From what security told me, he's just bumbling around. But—"

Freddy's hand grew impatient, tighter and tighter. He took the telephone with his free hand and slammed it once on the desk. Shake began to see orbs colliding when he told Gloria, in a small, strangled voice, "If he's no bother, just let him be. He paid to get in."

Freddy banged the telephone again. It gave a weak ring on impact.

"But, Mister Shake, he's—"

"Gloria—hi, Gloria, I'll have to get back to you." Shake dropped the intercom's extension back in the cradle, but it bounced. It lay on the table, rocking in place. Gloria's voice buzzed up.

"Mister Shake, he says he *knows* you."

He squashed the intercom extension against his ear.

"He said he what?"

"It's what park security *said*, Mister Shake. He told them he knew you."

It was what the little old man told security when they caught up with him, Dorothea and the bird. He waved his ticket stub, the one he found drifting in the parking lot when he wandered in. He arrived with the last of the pack when the bouffant women in the eight by eight gate stalls had grown too weary to rip every ticket and look every guest in the face.

Two new security men loomed over them on orders from Mister Shake to find "a man, white, aged somewhere in his eighties, accompanied by a small black and yellow bird—that talks."

"Well, he's kin. He's my great-great...great..." The little old man fumbled for greats—was it only two, or were there more?

The little bird made himself comfortable on Dorothea's shoulder, and from time to time, he caught a strand of her hair in his banana-yellow beak and watched it spring back.

Dorothea seethed. Two of the insect men had spied them both on the bench by the arcade. They flashed their badges in the good sheriff style in spite of their golfing trousers. Dorothea recognized the rounder of the men as the one who had tried to bribe her with chewing gum. And he did not remember her fondly; he hadn't needed stitches, but the ring of her teeth-marks throbbed alive as she bared an open-mouthed smile.

The little old man sat on this bench as comfortably as a transient would in a public park. The unwashed were unwelcome in these parts.

"You are kin to the park's publicist, sir? Well, wouldn't that make you one of the VIP?"

The insect men laughed; to Dorothea, they tittered, pretty snorts behind the hands and everything, much like little girls her age. She wondered if the older you grew (or the older you allowed yourself to grow), the more you had to reassure yourself that you were still funny.

She slipped her tiny hand into the little old man's papery one. She wouldn't allow him to be laughed at. His nails were talons, a whole crust of earth packed under them. He smiled ahead, not quite at them, but at the sliver of air between.

The doughy one pointed an inch away from Dorothea's nose. "Hey, you. Little girl."

She tried to imitate the old man's blankness, but she'd been caught. No sets of teeth were alike; the hammy guard lifted his thumb to show the ring of red craters that she, and no dog, had made. The black bird attempted peacemaking, crooning, "Don't be cruel!"

The doughy guard squinted. "You're one of the Novak kids, right? That uncle of yours around?"

Could she swing it, say that Uncle Freddy had suddenly become very old in the closing daylight?

"Is that a 'No'?"

She began to dig her nails into the old man's hand. She believed, or tried to believe, that it would be a 'Yes' if she welded herself to him, joined at the hand. Perhaps, then, they would disappear and leave them to look for her sister and her cousin in peace. Patience had become Tish again, and she dreaded that she would not be whole if she could not find her in time. Dorothea pictured her missing an arm or a leg, but that wasn't quite right.

Something sparked in the little old man then. His free hand quivered in its sleeve, and he gave an enraptured, *"Baaa!"* He struggled to his feet, lifting Dorothea with him. "Well, if this isn't a whole day of foot loosing! She's been telling me all about her people, she's been out herding them up, and I was just saying, you could try and whistle that old song about the St. Louis fair, and—Young lady, did you know I have a nephew hereabouts?"

The guards took a step closer. They spoke slowly, in the voice of the old to the toddlers at heart. "Mmm, she surely does. Your great-great-great-*gre-aaat-*nephew, that's right. And he sent us out here to take her to her people." Then, in a more adult tone to the little girl, "Your mothers didn't want a lot of commotion today, so Mister Teagarden's going to—"

"He's got my sister!" she bleated. It was all that could come out. What was happening to her?

"Right, and he's going to look after you—"

She could throw a tantrum right here. She'd never thrown one before, a keening, flat on the ground, leg-peddling display that would put a million reservations about taking her away into their heads. Her eyes welled.

"You come on with me, kiddo. Mickey, you wanna take care of Mister Shake's ol' granddad?"

The round one had her other wrist. The guard called Mickey had the old man's free hand. The old man, frightened, stiffened and his grip on Dorothea's hand was ironclad. The guards pulled, Dorothea found herself lifted up, her sandals scraping the pavement. The old man gibbered through his beard and this prompted the guard called Mickey to give a good wrench. The guests wandered in and out, heads turning dumbly at this tug-of-war.

And Dorothea screamed. A long, vibrating howl, for the ache in her shoulder; the clamminess in her hands; for her Uncle Freddy and the old man's tears; for her mother and her aunt (for her old ideas of them, that they would keep her within the magic circle); for ugly Mister Teagarden with his gnarled hands that went *crick-cruck*. She filled her lungs with a fresh howl.

The little bird took up the wail where Dorothea trailed off, circling the guards just above their heads, the little girl's skinned-alive rabbit cry going in and out of every pair of ears in its shot.

She felt her arms drop, and her knees met the ground. She tucked her hands under her armpits. She blinked. A blur, auburn halo around a pale moon. She blinked again, and let her eyes put the image together. She gaped, for here was Tish, her own sister, barefoot, her dress falling from the shoulder. Her sister who didn't groan when Dorothea clasped her arms around her. Yes, she was here and whole. Dorothea felt a shiver in her sister's arms, as though an icy current had blown through, and only Tish had caught it. She took Dorothea's hand and squeezed.

And Karen. She carried her sweater over one shoulder. Over the other, she dragged a bed sheet that whooshed spectrally behind her. She blinked. Then, as though every face in the crowd had come alive, had appeared out of the air, she was awake. Dropping the sheet with a cry she kicked it away. When the sheet flattened itself on the ground, a large spider poked its way through the folds. Its eight eyes twinkled, blue, yellow, pink, and then red from the lights. The sheet slithered over the pavement until one of the security men took it up in a pile to trap the spider within the layers and brought his foot down on it. Crunch. A little mournfully, he gathered it up and tipped it into the nearest trashcan.

Karen shuddered. "I hate spiders."

The little old man regained his bearings, backing into the bench. He looked to the sky, puckered his lips in a whistle. The song was "Camptown Races." The little bird reappeared and sat himself on the old man's shoulder, pecking at the flannel.

Patience began to fiddle with the button in her collar and allowed Dorothea to come around and fasten it for her.

"We had a whole bunch of things for you," Patience told Dorothea. "There was a Davy Crockett cap that I won at the Slap-a-Fish booth. I tried it on, and it was too tight, so I was going to give you that. And I got a ton of bead necklaces from one of the fortune teller midget ladies—I wanted to save the green ones for you, 'cause I know you like green. Karen won you this big stuffed strawberry thing. And I had a bag of gummy worms that I was going to split up with you when we got home—"

She stopped, looked around. For their mothers? Dorothea wondered. Then, with horror, for Mister Teagarden?

Karen came from the bush, brushing leaves. She sighed, a bit sadly. "Tish, I think they're gone. Those two—"

Patience swallowed and pressed her skirt against her legs, though there was no breeze to lift it.

Dorothea turned. The paths were lined with the guests who remained. The ladies crowded themselves around the children, a motherly tenderness settling over them like fairy dust. "Let me help you with that, dear. You just sit right down over there, right on this bench. I've got a little brush here, and we'll get those knots out. Such pretty hair you have—" The men prowled the circling ladies, alert to anything in the dark that might come lurking in. They stripped off their good blazers, wrapped them around the children's shoulders. "You came over looking shell-shocked. Are your folks near?"

Their folks. The children, all three, stared ahead, for their mothers, even their fathers, seemed too distant to think about, not like real people anymore but characters they'd said hello to in a dream. They couldn't have said why. When they went home that night, they each watched themselves in a slow disengagement from Lovey and Irene, refusing help to clean their ears with washcloths, change from good clothes into pajamas. The requests seemed so foreign now, but the children told their mothers calmly that they didn't need help. When they closed their doors at bedtime, they locked them. In the privacy of their separate kitchens, Irene and Lovey wept mascara-clogged tears onto the tablecloths, hands clawed in their hair. So, it wasn't so easy, after all; their children had not come away unspoiled. The knowledge of what might have happened to them in Teagarden's care was theirs now. A voice, deep in their bowels, told this to each of the sisters. *All yours now.*

Dorothea flopped her arms in the big sleeves, a men's blazer like an army overcoat. She wasn't cold, and so she went to Karen, who had been staring into the darkness. Far away, the lights blinked, green, then red, then pink, then yellow, the rides running a final lap before the park closed.

Dorothea waved the blazer.

Karen took it and slid her arms through the sleeves.

Dorothea took her hand. "Karen? Who's gone?"

chapter 17

About one hour ago in the Condor's Lair, the old bird clawed the moss from his perch, watched it fall to the layer of wood chips in flakes. His feet itched. The moss was fabric stuff around a plaster branch—he'd shat on it, and Ranger Dale pounded the chicken-wire mesh around the cage with his hand. This was Ranger Dale at his most rugged, an overgrown Cub Scout with a bald spot. He asked the old bird questions, which was funny because the only questions he could ever answer were his own. Those asked by the kids were too precise. He knew the old bird couldn't tell his tiny audience *exactly how* he hunted sea lions or *exactly why* condor eggs were a little blue and not plain white.

Ranger Dale snatched up the surplus bag of wood chips and a rag. "You couldn't *wait* for me to clean this hole out first?" He slammed a bucket into the sink across the way from the cage and filled it a quarter of the way, one part water, one part something blue from a carton, to eat away the brown stains in the moss, and, unintentionally, the skin of the old bird's feet. "Do you know when I take off? You know, take off?" He brought his hands up to his shoulders and flapped them clownishly. "Five minutes. You know what'll happen to those five minutes? All gone because it turns into sixty minutes, getting this shit sanitary! What, you got something to say to me?"

The old bird nudged his beak between his feathers and began to groom, eyeing Ranger Dale stomp the concrete in his pressed khaki shorts. The registered forest ranger was plump in his uniform, thinly furred on the arms and head. The old bird told himself about the virtues of patience. Let the meat come to you. A beefy finger flipped the latch, and Ranger Dale lumbered in, dragging the wood chips, the bucket.

It was a sad end for Ranger Dale: The old bird spent the night in a basement cage, twelve feet underground. And so, anyone topside made out a squeak, only a squeak. The old bird lapped at his talons and dug into the split flesh of Ranger Dale's neck. The best feed he'd had in months.

Twelve feet above, Walter and Sonia hurried down the path from the Condor's Lair. They had come back for their things. They'd told each other, to hell with addressing the big boss. They would pack up, they would collect their things and disappear into the sunset.

Walter had little else besides his incredible food supply. He'd made a quick rummage through the

Rattleback's operating room. He carried a toolkit. It was his own, he said, at least the tools inside were: a screwdriver, an industrial flashlight, a thick roll of electrical tape, a set of needle-nose pliers. Sonia kept a spare change of clothes in the Children's Cottage; the nanny there promised to look after them until the end of the day when Sonia could change and have the park's clothing laundered.

Neither of them had a key to the cottage. They went around to a little alley where the stink of the restrooms beside them was the most foul. But at last, a window, so nicely out of the way.

"Wouldn't it look a bit suspicious?" Sonia asked in their native German. "We might be thrown out for stealing."

"Nonsense," Walter told her. "They couldn't throw anyone out for taking what already belongs to us already."

He pulled at the window. He put his weight into it, all one-hundred-and-thirty pounds. Sonia giggled, a hand over her mouth.

Bomp, bomp. Walter's hands flew away from the glass. Had the cottage nanny been in all along?

Bomp, bomp, bomp, bomp! The lacy curtain flew aside to a girl's face, damp with sweat, her auburn hair plastered in strips to her forehead. To call her a little girl would not quite fit: Her chipmunk cheeks had begun to thin. She looked about eleven, maybe twelve. Her face flushed grey and red in the waning light, from tears she wouldn't let spill. She put her finger to her lips and pulled the curtain farther aside. Sonia and Walter peered in.

The window began to fog, thin, as though for a second time. The girl wiped it away with the ham of her hand, and Sonia and Walter waited for their eyes to adjust to the dark. Another girl, a little younger and with the same auburn hair, huddled, lumped in a single sheet to the edge of a child's bed. Both girls had slipped with haste into their shoes, the fasteners flapping open. The socks and sweaters were forgotten on the floor along with, if Sonia squinted, a small pile of prizes, Mardi Gras beads, a coonskin cap, bags of sweets, a little satiny pillow shaped like a strawberry. The girls edged in tiny steps to the window. Their eyes were trained to something just out of sight, at the far end of the room that might wake if disturbed.

The older girl was back again at the window. She knotted her fists together, and showed Sonia and Walter a thrusting motion lightly against the glass.

Sonia ducked out, came back with a piece of brick. She reared her hand back. *Like this?*

A nod from the girl. Quickly, she rubbed the steam away from the glass. She flapped her hand for the others to stand back.

When they did, Walter showed them his face, hands over his eyes. They aped him.

The glass cracked, a spider web in the center of the round window, then, one more heave and it shattered, chips sparking into the darkness of the cottage. A waft of clammy air sighed out, tinged with the fetor of body. The children's faces steamed when they crept to the window and then froze. A moist sound, a beastly grunting from the floor. Then silence.

Walter lifted the girls out, easing them over the broken glass. The older of them cast an eye to the far end of the room, from where the wet animal grunt had come. When it came again, louder this time, she turned and heaved herself out. Once in the alley, she grasped Sonia's wrist and whispered fiercely, "He's asleep. *Don't* wake him up."

"You are hurt?" Sonia pronounced.

The girl pulled up her dress by the collar. "No. I don't think so. We were asleep for...Well, for a few hours. He got so angry when we said we wanted to find Uncle Freddy. We said we wanted to go home. He said we couldn't go home until he said we could. Because we're Ickacks now, he said. *Because we're Ickacks now.* Oh, I don't even know what that means..."

She turned on her heel and ran to where the younger girl stood behind a row of trashcans, grappling for the sheet that whipped out behind her in the gathering nighttime winds. The girls wrapped themselves in the sheet with a humility that may have only dawned upon them moments before Sonia's and Walter's arrival. They spared no time mourning a dead paradise. They scattered into the park, a pounding of tiny feet echoing into the air that grew still and cool.

Sonia watched them go, and a blur of Hamburg memory surfaced. A family, mother, sons, father, crawling one by one from a hole in the wall of a building. Or was it a window? They emerged into the street laden with suitcases and disappeared as quick as a blink.

Out in the world, Walter and Sonia would have their happily-ever-after. Walter took a job as a car mechanic in Berkeley, and Sonia took in sewing. Though, many nights for years after, both would try to scrub from their memories their first steps in America. The most unrelenting of all came in the frame of a broken window into a heavy, dark room crammed with plush toys. A hog-like grunt shuddered from a rocking chair, where a sleeping man, white and writhing like a maggot in a fine linen suit, grunted and swayed, his heels dragging against the carpet.

And he was awake with a jerk, a shuddering motion through his whole body. He glanced around, then growled. The children were gone. Hands batting the air, then an inflatable clown, sweat misting from his flesh in clouds when he decided that the clown was to blame. It laughed with each punch in a high, rubbery voice. Sonia and Walter watched, horrified, as Teagarden drummed a pow-wow with his fists, until they bounced back and clubbed him in the nose. It surprised him as much as it did his audience, who stood peering through the round window like visitors at a zoo.

Teagarden shivered. The night air was settling in a thick layer over the hothouse cottage, and the plush animals sighed. And whether it was the shock of the cool air or the rage that had come through him in a gust, it took him an extra breath to fill his lungs. The world had gotten very close, his chest very tight. A burning in his neck. It lapped down his left arm, eating Teagarden in a flame that no one but he could see. He hissed through his teeth, the spittle on his chin.

And then he saw the Germans. So thin, the flickering from the restroom lamps gave them both the look of two skulls in the dark come for Teagarden. He dropped from the rocking chair to his hands, brought his legs together. He gulped the air like water, tearing the linen blazer from his shoulders, grappling with the knot in his tie. The floor was closer than before. The lamps flickered, and the skulls were back. Far off, somewhere in the back of his head, he heard a chorus of high voices, cackling witches, or kids skipping rope in the street:

> *The worms crawl in, the worms crawl out*
> *The worms play pinochle in your snout*

He went to his knees again, hands flat and bearing the trembling meat of him. Sweat and spittle dripped in runners from his nose. His chest felt whole sizes too small for his heart. Had it grown, or had he shrunk in this steaming little cottage? *The worms crawl in...*

The Germans were sure they heard correctly. Teagarden gasped, "This whole thing. It's not my fault."

He dropped. Famous last words.

chapter 18

"*H*ey!"

Shake made a sorry entrance, but he dragged himself forward, pressing a reddening handkerchief to a nose that dripped generously.

The man in his wake, the new Freddy Novak, parted the crowds as he ran for his nieces. They clamored for their Uncle Freddy, a mass of arms and hands that wished for him to bring them all back to the way it had all been, before the park, before they had all become part of the notorious Ickack family. Freddy gathered up Patience, grasped Dorothea's hand, kissed Karen. They clung to each other, this single mass of beating hearts.

"*Hey!* Hey, you!" Shake barked. He jabbed a finger at the bench. "You!"

The little old man had been looking on peacefully, happy as a spectator with his little black bird, perched atop his shining head. He plucked a corner of his flannel shirt.

Shake's eyes bulged, road mapped with veins. He staggered closer, his fingers a pistol. *"You—will—leave these—premises—right—now."*

The little man blinked. Then, he let fall the filthy corner of his shirt so that he could spread and fold Shake into an embrace smelling of earthworms. "Arnold, Arnold Nathanael Schacherstein!" he wept into Shake's linen shoulder. "I din' believe it when I read it in the papers. Not my Arnold, it couldn't be. I don' believe it if I can' see it. Name in the papers an' everything! Look at you, what you made yourself into!" He laughed, a geezer's "Hee-heee!" straight from the nose.

Shake clapped his arms to his sides, his visage chalky. He swallowed the first deferred vomit. He took the little man by the lapels, and it was no effort to get him moving, bony ankles dragging on the pavement. The little bird squawked like a dying accordion; the old man gibbered and wept, for it was all mixed up with the blinking lights and new faces and would no one help him?

Freddy pursed his lips. *"Arnold Nathanael Schacherstein."* He tasted the words. Before he could think, he watched himself strutting up to the old man, grasping his shoulders, telling him in the gentlest of voices, "There, there, Uncle Ely. You're just a little excited, is all. It's me, you remember me, don't you?

Little Freddy? Your *nephew*, you know me. Don't get us confused, now."

The old man's knees knocked together, his eyes shone. The little bird tapped its claws blissfully across his skull. He calmed himself into Freddy's hands, shifting the bones into his palms. Freddy pictured a sheep at his side, and knew him at once. His photo hung in his apartment, his sisters' homes with the reverence of a shrine.

It would be Shake's final ruin, and perhaps the park's, too. But the day had been long, and those before it seemed to meld with it into one hideous nightmare. The lights from the rides blinked constellations of pink, yellow, red, green. Now was the time to bring this day to and end. Freddy clapped a hand on Shake's shoulder.

"Now, now, now!" he said, "Mister Shake, let's not be so hasty. *You* don't recognize this man?"

The crowd murmured, overlapping in white noise.

Shake paled, more bloodless than typing paper. "Don't you dare—"

"I certainly do. If you can't see a surefire kin resemblance, I can." Freddy grinned. He strolled to the little old man, who had been stroking the little bird's bristling feathers, and draped an arm over his shoulders.

"Perhaps I should reiterate," Freddy chortled. "I meant between him and I. You see, everyone—" he clapped a hand on the little old man's shoulder, bringing up a poof of road dust "—I'd wanted to introduce the *whole* family, this man by my side. Arnold, well—I brought Uncley Ely into the office one day, and Arnold would have nothing to do with him! Not that he would tell my old uncle to his face. So he takes me aside, he tells me, 'He's case-study dementia, Freddy! Futzing around in the mountains when you should have stuck him in a home. Look into his eyes now, he's dead already.' "

The crowd gaped. The old folks, in wheelchairs, hobbling on canes, cast wet looks at their grown-up children, then at Shake. The grown up children, thirty, forty, fifty years old, gnashed their teeth—the very thought! Evil it was, a sweet little man holed away in a home!

Shake closed his eyes. If he couldn't see them, they couldn't see him.

Freddy went on, the old man wrapped in the arm of the younger one, baffled but grinning. "Look into his eyes now, he's dead already," Freddy spat. "I couldn't get that out of my mind, and I'll never forgive myself. Because I saw him the way Shake did then: He couldn't even remember his name, let alone the pleasure garden. I showed him the Jacob's Ladder, the one from Granddaddy, and he gurgled, asked me when the big bird would be coming back. 'Where is Mother?' he asked me. 'Where is she?' He was gone to us. But would I let the park go to waste? I couldn't break a promise now. I'd like to think that it was wholly out of that promise. And, Uncle Ely, I hope you can forgive me. I guess this is as good a time as any for a confession—" He bowed his head, let his lips quiver.

"—Shake and I knew a good thing when we saw it. Shake said to me, he said, 'Has he got a lawyer?' I didn't know what he was getting at. My uncle never did trust attorneys. Shake said, 'Has he got a will?' I'd seen it, the whole family had. Our parents liked to speculate what our cut was going to be. Our cut, like they were talking about meat. Shake said, 'Well, the old man's not exactly keeping an eye on it.' And, Lord help me, but I thought, 'You know, he's right. The old man's so out to lunch, he doesn't know who he is anymore. It's not such a bad thing,' I was thinking, 'it's not as if I'm taking all the credit for this venture, is it?' "

Freddy stopped. He worked his face like clay, drawing it all in toward the tip of his nose, such agony he nearly, honestly, felt it. Perhaps he would win his Oscar, after all. The crowd wept with him, a little lady wheeled to him, patted his hand. "There, there dear." He daubed his nose with his sleeve. Then the old man reached a hand to Freddy's face (to catch the salt), and all hearts warmed. It was a sign of absolution, they thought.

"And now, he wants to throw my uncle out? *My uncle?*" Freddy had never barked before, the ache in his throat was astonishing. The old man yelped.

The crowd knotted closer, putting the equation of the two men's faces together. They let their imaginations process the best, if most incorrect, work they could. They found family resemblance—in the eyes, the shapes of the noses, the jaws, —that was not there. They gnashed their teeth at Shake, suddenly loathsome, meat in the lion's den. The young boys in the crowd took up a mantra that had a raucous, singsong rhythm: "Shake's for shit, Shake's for shit, I-think-it-looks-like Shake's for shit…" All these people came from decent homes and tried to recall how their Savior talked about casting the first stone. But the Old Testament was much more satisfying: eye for an eye. No one would say it aloud, but the single thought circulated as they closed in on Arnold Shake, ladies clasping their purses like clubs, the men ripping open their shirt cuffs to push up the sleeves, boys wielding whiffle ball bats, girls swinging their mammoth dollies by the ankles.

This left Arnold Shake in a bad place. No, the crowd was not too old for tantrums. They, these grown ups and their children, had to fend for themselves in a world where dreams normally did not come true. Didn't they deserve the tiny pleasures of a manmade paradise? The lights, the abundance of food battered and grilled and fudge-topped, the rewards you took despite your poor aim or bad eye—they had to protect all that somehow. And one little fluke could kill the dream forever. There was no goodness here— little pleasures were made with a little heart in every bit, as home cooked meals were. Hadn't this place been advertised as such—a home away from home?

Freddy had forgiveness, for the old man's hand on his face showed them that.

Shake, blackened, vile Shake, flapping his hands, sputtering as they all loomed over him, hissing and spitting. One of the on-the-road brides whipped her veil from her head, the pins inside the band striking sparks in the streetlight. Four more brides followed, making a row of pins like bayonets.

And, for Shake, the world caved in. First came the layer of children delivering blows with bats and dolls. The ones who had a knack for the target games brought out their prizes of slingshots, taking aim with pebbles and hard candies. Then their mothers: Their purses were heavy and they dropped them into Shake's face, hidden by hands pecked open by the pebbles. The men heard the snap (Shake's nose) turn into an orchestra of clicks as the bones splintered, the scream of the man buried alive under his new enemies. They braved the blows from purses, tossed aside their own children to get at him, the man who charged them five dollars a pop to get into this place like it meant nothing at all, and here he was cutting the heart out of it. Shake's corpus was putty in their beefy hands; the skin split thickly, and there came more glorious crunches when they had him underfoot. Stiletto heels, brogue toes, the ribs split like kindling. Make him road kill. The kids loved the word, and stamped a tattoo in time. Dollies were raised high, lace blood-spattered and curls wild. *"Roadkill! Roadkill! Roadkill!"* Shake's eyes, swollen shut, saw them as foggy pumpkin heads, and the children's mantra filled in what the purpled lids closed out: All mouth, sweaty teeth, laughter sparking up their forms, heads bulging.

They fell away, the kill bright against their Sunday best. All was quiet; it came so, so fleetingly that it was as though they had only watched from afar while these other selves, the barbarous infants, did their worst. It took five minutes. But there lay Arnold Shake, né Arnold Shacherstein, a forty-year-old pancake. A miracle had been granted in the fracas, in that he was still alive. The suit dampened, crimson and grey with blood, ridged where the bones lumped. His skin was blackened with the gritty imprints of shoes, puckering around high heel stomps. The tip of his nose touched his right eyelid, his lips flat, run through with pieces of broken teeth. The word "Keds" would be a permanent mark on his face.

Freddy's kids remained out of the loop in the attack. The little old man staggered forward, to scrape at what was left of Arnold Shake. With steady hands, he went through his coat, and removed a paper bag from an inside pocket. He stooped to the body, and into the bag went a jacket button and four teeth. The crowd, trembling with the rush of what they had done, allowed room for this small ceremony—the real Ickack, they thought, mourning for the man who took their dollars and, very nearly, their ending to a beautiful day. Freddy's kids let out a collective breath. The day had become too real. When Dorothea read of it in the next morning's issue of *The L.A. Times*, she would search for all that had really happened as she had never needed to do with the stories in *True Crime*.

Freddy turned to the little old man, his eyes glowing with the glory of a lifetime, or the joy of a long-lost homecoming, take your pick. He enveloped the little man in an embrace, full of wet earth and relief and confusion, and said, loud enough for all to hear, "Uncley Ely, how we've missed you. You've come back to us, Elijah Ickack. Welcome home."

Evette Jonquil kept her 1919 Rolls Royce parked on the other side of the highway. There was a sightseeing venue where travelers could pull over and look out onto the mustard hills. The park snaked over the gold and green leaves, whirring and glowing with candy lights.

Every so often, and then with horrible frequency, she gathered voices that were distinctly, ferociously human. *"Roadkill! Roadkill! Roadkill!"*

She ground the ignition. The car sputtered and would not go. Up the hill the voices came, louder and without substance.

Panicked, Miss Jonquil tore the mink coat from her shoulders and threw it out the window. "Take it! Just take it! Leave me be! Please, please!"

When she moved to pry the door open, there, perched on the hood of the car, was a small, black bird. It opened its beak, bleating, "Roadkill!" into the heat.

Acknowledgements

My husband, Michael. My parents, Carol Compton Hopkins, Scott and Debra Hopkins. My brothers. My cousins. My Division 3 team at Hampshire College in 2011, where this book was first written as my senior thesis. To Veronica Bane for taking a chance on me. To Nate Ragolia for resurrecting this book. To Jarrod Campbell, Tex Gresham, and Hillary Leftwich for blurbing. Thank you.

About the Author

Pam Jones was born in 1989 and raised on the East Coast. She now lives in Austin, Texas with her husband. She studied creative writing at Hampshire College and is at work on her next book. She released *The Biggest Little Bird* with Black Hill Press/1888 Center, and *Andermatt County: Two Parables* with The April Gloaming. Her short fiction has appeared in *The Cost of Paper* and *Boned: A Collection of Skeletal Fiction*.

About the Publishing Team

Nate Ragolia is a lifelong lover of science fiction and its power to imagine worlds more hopeful and inclusive than the real one. His first book, *There You Feel Free*, was published by 1888's Black Hill Press in 2015. Spaceboy Books reissued it in 2021. He's also the author of *The Retroactivist* (2017). His most recent book, *One Person Can't Make a Difference* (2022), was featured on Tor.com's Can't Miss Indie Press Speculative Fiction list, and was translated into Italian for Ringworld Sci-Fi in 2023. He founded and edited *BONED*, a literary magazine, and also created two webcomics. Nate is also a husband and a dog dad.

Shaunn Grulkowski has been compared to Warren Ellis and Phillip K. Dick and was once described as what a baby conceived by Kurt Vonnegut and Margaret Atwood would turn out to be. He's at least the fifth best Slavic-Latino-American sci-fi writer in the Baltimore metro area. He's the author *Retcontinuum*, and the editor of *A Stalled Ox* and *The Goldfish* for 1888/Black Hill Press.